WINE COUNTRY KING

CALIFORNIA SUITS, BOOK TWO

CLAIRE MARTI

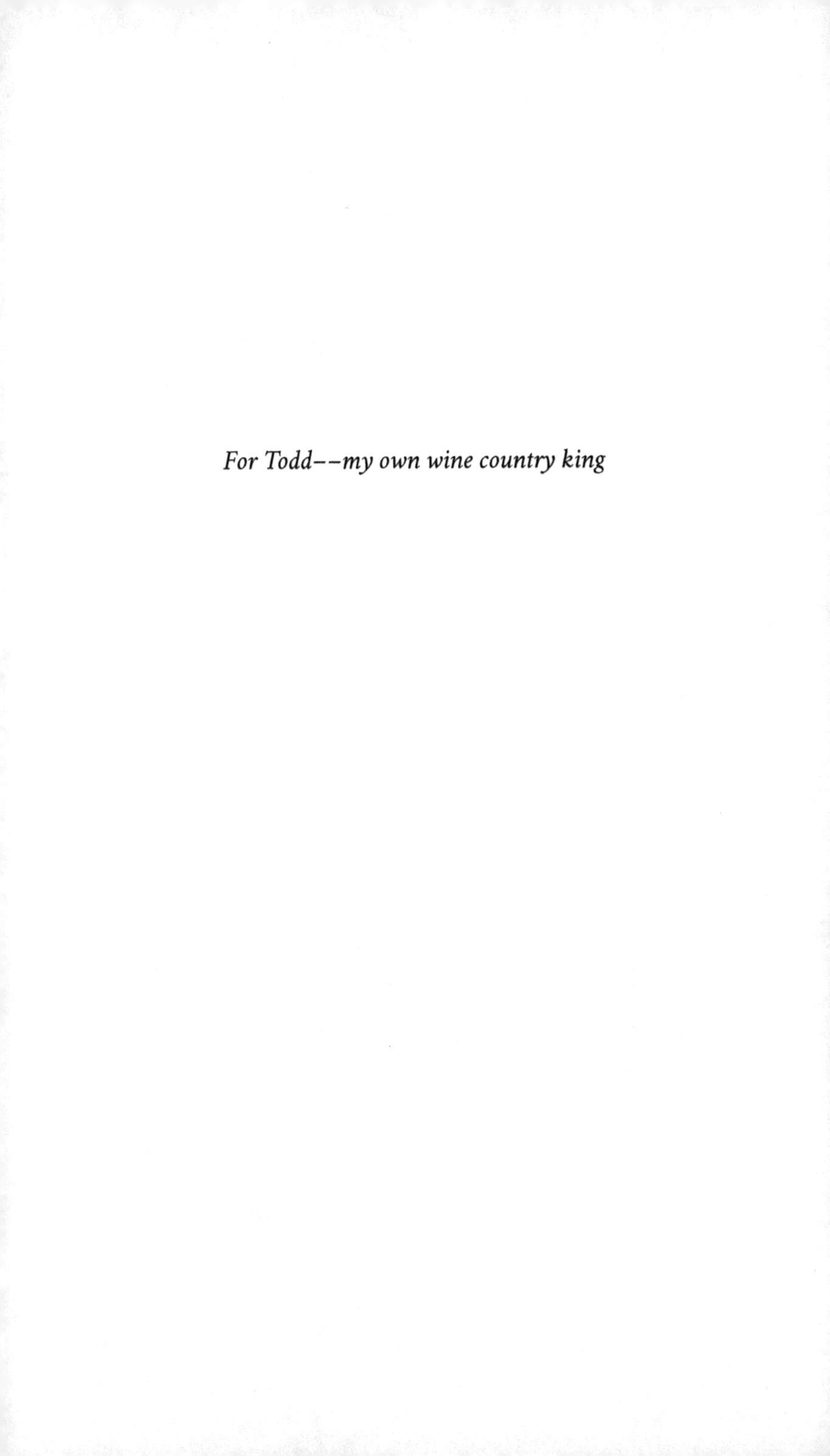

For Todd--my own wine country king

CHAPTER 1

The moment when Campbell Taylor first laid eyes on Jack Cassidy, her heart performed a double cartwheel, triple back flip. She was sure one day they'd ride off into the sunset and live happily ever after.

Seventeen years later, reality hadn't aligned with her teenaged fantasies.

Yes, they were working together every day to open Maison du Soleil.

Sure, Jack was parking his sleek silver Range Rover in front of her rented duplex, where they would reside together for the next few months.

And that was her current dilemma––Jack believed he was moving into his own one-bedroom apartment, not sharing hers.

When he learned she'd taken the liberty of breaking his short-term lease without consulting him, the odds of him being aggravated were high. Despite his charming, easy-going demeanor, he was an intense real estate attorney reputed to always negotiate the best deal for his clients and losing his living space without his consent wouldn't sit well.

Once she explained the circumstances to Jack, he'd be cooperative. *Keep telling yourself that.*

No need to be nervous––Jack was a level-headed guy. She wiped her damp palms along her jeans, squared her shoulders, and whipped open the front door. She shielded her eyes from the penetrating California sun beating down from the cloudless blue sky. September in Paso Robles ran hot––as evidenced by the sheen of sweat that glued the back of her thin cotton tank top to her skin. With a fortifying breath, she waved and sauntered outside.

No way could she allow her landlord, their landlord, to break the news to Jack first. "You made it." There, that sounded normal, not like the cry of a panic-stricken woman, right?

He unfolded his lean, muscular frame clad in dark denim and a crisp white button-down from the SUV. His square-jawed face split into that familiar crooked grin, his eyes shrouded behind mirrored aviators. "You planning on helping me unload my stuff?"

The wide gravel path crunched beneath her low-heeled boots as Campbell crossed the postage stamp yard separating them. "Something like that." She swallowed the nerves fluttering up her throat. "Let's go inside first."

Jack's dark brows drew together. "Is something wrong?"

"Not exactly. It's sweltering out here, so come inside and I'll explain." She turned and strode toward the building. Their landlord Kyle's house was across the palm-tree-lined courtyard, and she wanted to ward him off, at least until she'd explained the situation.

Jack shrugged one broad shoulder and fell into step next to her. "You're acting weird."

She looked up at him. "Not weird. There's been a change in the living arrangements, and I prefer to discuss it in the air-conditioning."

They entered the small yet charming condo she'd been calling home for the last few months. It was essentially one room, with a wood-beamed ceiling, wide-plank floors, and a butcher block kitchen island dividing the space. She'd adorned the ivory walls with colorful reproductions of Monet and Manet paintings, two of the artists she'd fallen for during her year abroad studying in Paris.

Jack sat in the honey-colored leather armchair and hooked his sunglasses on his shirt collar. "What's going on?"

She perched on the edge of the soft plum-colored velvet couch across from him and the words tumbled out. "So, our landlord's father is ill. He couldn't stay in assisted living and refused to start hospice care in the middle of his son's tiny living room. When Kyle told me about it, I told him you and I could share my condo since he knew we were practically family. I figured you'd agree once you learned about the situation."

Jack massaged the back of his neck and sighed. "Wow. Okay, that's a tough one. But Paso Robles is at full occupancy because of harvest season and this place only has one bedroom, right? And we aren't family, Campbell."

Her cheeks heated. "I know, but I figured since there's a Murphy bed in here, you'd be okay with sharing my place. As soon as harvest ends, something should open up. And you were planning on buying a house up here anyway, right?"

Jack's jaw tightened, but to his credit, his voice remained the same whiskey smooth baritone. "I'm not house hunting during these last few months before opening the hotel, no. And your brother isn't going to be thrilled at the idea of us sharing a place."

She snorted and rolled her eyes. "Cameron knows I'm a 32-year-old woman and hardly need a chaperone. Especially with you."

Jack's full lips turned down at the corners. "Especially with me? What's that supposed to mean?"

Campbell laughed. "Are you offended? You're basically my honorary big brother and you used to stay at our house all the time. I think we can handle being roommates." As long as she could keep her secret attraction to him under wraps. Which had seemed a lot simpler before his larger-than-life personality and six-foot something of deliciousness dominated the condo.

"I haven't had a roommate in over a decade. There's got to be another solution." He surged to his feet and stalked to the other side of the room, where rustic bookshelves framed a matching faux barn door. He tugged on the wrought iron handles and unveiled his sleeping accommodations. "And a Murphy bed? It's like something out of the last century."

She smoothed back the pesky strand of hair escaping from her ponytail and huffed out a breath. "This place is lovely, and it's been fully remodeled. Surely you can adapt to pulling down a queen-sized bed from the wall."

He turned and smirked at her. "Yes, I am capable of pulling the bed down. I just don't want to."

Laughter bubbled up in her throat. "You look like a toddler who was sent to his room without a bedtime story. Stop pouting."

He stuck out his tongue and sank onto the mattress, which creaked under his weight. "We're two executives opening a luxury destination retreat on York Mountain, catering to some of the most exclusive wine lovers in the world, and we're sharing a miniature condo?"

She wrinkled her nose. "Well, when you put it like that. Look, I'm sorry. I just blurted it out and couldn't renege. We won't be here much anyway, right? And at least it isn't a sofabed. If it bugs you so much, you can sleep in the bedroom, and I'll sleep out here." Although the vision of him stretched out on her eyelet comforter caused her mouth to go dry. Maybe he was right, and this was a terrible idea.

He narrowed his almost translucent green eyes. "I know it's the right thing to do but it's not ideal. Though, between you studying for the Master Sommelier exam, and all the work that needs to be done on Maison du Soleil, you're right about our time being limited here. Under any other circumstances, I'd insist he give me the other place."

She exhaled a steadying breath. Hurdle cleared. "This is unusual for sure and yes, it will be a little tight. There's space in the closet and Kyle moved in an additional dresser for you."

He rose and made an elaborate show of replacing the barn door. "Fine. But I'm not conceding defeat. I'm going to make some calls and see if I can find something else. I'll bring in my suitcases, but I'm not unpacking yet."

"All you brought was a few suitcases?"

He shrugged and turned toward the door. "I put my furniture in storage in San Diego since *my* apartment was supposed to be furnished. I've got some boxes of books and other stuff which I'll leave in the car, but you know I travel light."

"I thought you'd grown out of that. But it makes sense." Her heart softened. Jack had always been a bit of a nomad.

Back when her brother was a freshman at San Diego State, he'd brought Jack home for Thanksgiving and her family basically took him in as a second son. Because his military parents were stationed overseas and rarely returned to the States, he'd spent most holidays with them ever since.

When eighteen-year-old Jack had stepped across the threshold of her childhood home, Campbell had only been fifteen, a true tomboy focused more on winning soccer tournaments than kissing boys. He'd flashed his straight white teeth, winked at her, and greeted her with a "hey, kid."

Her adrenaline had skyrocketed like when she'd drive down the soccer field, and in that instant, she'd finally understood why her two best friends gushed about certain boys.

Jack's smooth light brown skin, dark wavy hair, and striking beach glass eyes made him the most beautiful person she'd ever seen. Jack had been lankier then, before he and Cameron dove into weightlifting with a vengeance during their ROTC training. He'd treated her like a little sister, but she'd worshiped him like a rock star.

In secret, of course. No way would she have risked her brother's teasing her or even worse, the humiliation of Jack learning of her infatuation. As far as he knew, her primary focus was on earning good grades so she could win a scholarship to UC Berkeley because she sure wasn't going into the Army like her brother. Thank goodness he'd lived hundreds of miles away in San Diego or she probably would have flunked out.

"Earth to Campbell." Jack waved one wide-palmed hand in front of her face. "I'll grab my stuff and then we can head over to York Mountain. You're joining me for the meeting with the contractors, right?"

She snapped back to the present. "I am. I want to make sure they're on track for the wine cellar. Maybe I should drive separately, though, because I've got to hit the books."

"No, let's ride together, that way I can give you more crap for terminating my lease. And we can catch up on the way. I'll drop you back. Where do you do most of your studying, by the way?" He looked around the apartment, his dark brows knit together over his strong straight nose.

"It depends. Sometimes here, sometimes with my study group out at Salis Farms Winery, and other times the library." And she'd probably be living at the library because no way could she focus on terroir and appellations with him close by.

He shook his head. "Yeah, I'll be in the way here. I'm going to see if I can call in a few favors. There's got to be another solution."

Like she hadn't spent hours calling around to everyone she knew already. "It will all work out. Grab your stuff and I'll gather my hotel notebook. Ready to go in 5?"

His sculpted lips tightened but he nodded and strode out the door.

Campbell's shoulders sagged and she exhaled an unsteady breath. Every single cell of her being craved his touch. She must be out of her mind to believe she could hide her years-old crush from him. Time to toughen up, buttercup.

CHAPTER 2

*J*ack forced his gaze to remain on the winding road and his focus on the upcoming contractor meetings at Maison du Soleil. But the rich floral scent of Campbell's long, shiny hair was too tantalizing. If it weren't so damn hot today, he'd open the windows.

The rolling golden hills and green-dotted valleys whizzed by, a stark contrast to the bowl of blue sky and wide lanes of Highway 46. The York Mountain wine region, where they were launching the second Hotel Kings LLC boutique hotel, sat on the western edge of Paso Robles, just miles from the Pacific Ocean. Something about this area of central California tugged at him in a way he'd never experienced, which is why he'd insisted he be the one to manage Maison du Soleil.

Because it was a planned green hotel and needed to pass the stringent LEED Platinum Certification, the remodeling phase was crucial and no shortcuts or mistakes could occur. Sure, marrying luxury and environmental values wouldn't be easy, but the end result would be worth every extra minute of effort. For the next few hours, he needed to be on top of his game.

But damn it, his mind couldn't focus on wine or wood milled from salvaged trees and solar panels right now. His senses were full of Campbell. At Pacific Jewel Inn's opening earlier in the month, he'd been unable to ignore that his buddy's smart-ass tomboy sister had transformed into a brilliant, talented woman. Granted, her sass hadn't dissipated, and her quick wit remained one of his favorite qualities about her. But now they were working together, and his attraction to her was a problem.

He gritted his teeth and white-knuckled the steering wheel to prevent reaching out to stroke her bare arm to see if her skin was as silky as it looked. Impulse control wasn't one of his issues. Usually.

Sharing a tiny apartment would never work. Although he understood why the always compassionate Campbell had offered to help, she'd created a potential firestorm of tempting moments. Like her taking a shower or sliding under her sheets with only a thin wall and a few feet separating them. Every muscle in his body tensed and he shifted in his seat.

"We need to keep the living situation a secret."

"What? Seriously?" Her pale pink lips parted.

"Seriously. If the guys find out I don't have my own place and am crashing on your couch, they'll assume I'm not in it for the long haul." Hell, the Hotel Kings were his best friends and yet, they regularly gave him crap about his revolving door of women, jobs, and cities.

She shook her head. "That's ridiculous. Everyone knows you're perfect for this role and staying with me is temporary."

"Exactly. Temporary. Actions speak louder than words. Nobody will believe I'm going to stick in Paso until I'm here for a few years. I'd rather not deal with it." He'd sworn to Ryan he was making the transition from full time attorney to Managing Director/General Counsel.

She pulled off her sunglasses and shifted to face him, her brow creased. "Don't sell yourself short."

His heart tightened in his chest. "You're a sweetheart. But Cam is protective of you, too, and won't like it." Not to mention Cameron thought he was a player.

"Oh please. You and Cam are best friends, and it would be ridiculous for him to be worried about that. Everyone knows you're part of the family. I mean, my parents always say your last name should be Cassidy-Taylor."

His lips curved up. The Taylors truly *were* like family. Another reason he needed to maintain boundaries. Campbell might still look at him like a sibling, but his feelings were anything but fraternal. Sharing an apartment would only make matters worse. Not the ideal way to start this new phase in his life.

He jolted when she laid one long slender hand on his forearm.

Her full blonde eyebrows rose. "Okay, jumpy. What do you propose?"

He blew out a breath. "Sorry. There's no reason for anyone to know and it would make my life easier and avoid drama, okay?"

She tapped two fingers against her unpainted mouth. "I didn't mean to complicate things but maybe you have a point."

He dragged his eyes away from those tempting lips and focused on the road. "I usually do. Opening Maison du Soleil is priority number one. We can't afford any delays or external issues if we're going to open the hotel by the December deadline."

"We can't. Okay. I'll be buried this time next week and I can't fail the theory exam again."

"I'm sorry you didn't pass. I heard that test is a beast." He glanced at her.

"It was brutal. Most candidates take it two to three times, but I thought I'd be the exception and pass on the first round. Shows me for being too cocky." She shrugged one slender shoulder and frowned. "And I can't take the second two exams on practical restaurant and wine services and practical tasting until I pass theory. I can't choke again."

"I can't imagine you choking on an exam. You aced the Advanced Sommelier exam, right?" She was a fierce competitor--one thing that hadn't changed from when he'd first met her as a teenaged soccer star and high school Valedictorian.

She nodded and smoothed back her silver-blonde ponytail. "Yeah, well imagine if the Bar exam had an oral portion with judges hammering you with questions like tennis balls being pelted at you from an automated machine. On top of that, you're supposed to be charming and social while they're trying to trip you up with esoteric questions on shale and limestone."

He shuddered. "Yeah, I remember moot court from law school. No thanks. I've got no idea how you can sip wine and know what region and year the grape is from--I mean, I consider myself a wine connoisseur, but your abilities boggle the mind."

She shifted in her seat toward him. "I love it all so much--ever since that first wine dinner in Paris, I was hooked. My palate is lucky, but the memorization is intense. I've been at this for ten years and trust me, I feel like I've earned my doctorate in wine. But it's uber-competitive. And I'm competing with some real charmers who will do anything to become part of the Court of Master Sommeliers."

"Charmers?" He glanced over again; her sarcasm was impossible to ignore.

Her delicate triangular jaw was tight. "The egos in this business are massive. There's about a 10% pass rate at the top level and candidates want to get in with 5-star hotels or Michelin star restaurants, so it's a tiny pool. My mentor is awesome though and he helps me stay focused on what's important, but I've got a real piece of work in my local study group."

"If it's your passion, then do whatever you need to do to make your dreams come true. You'd be bored if it was too easy, right? And let me know if you need me to take anyone out for you." He smirked and shook a fist, wanting to soften the line that formed between her brows.

She laughed, just like he'd wanted her to. "Now you're the sweetheart. Yeah, you can go rough up those bullies for me."

"Only if you help me get these contractors to move faster." He'd been working with the foreman long-distance but now that he would be on-site daily, the pace *would* pick up.

"Oh yeah, I'm sure they'll listen to me. You know I stop by and get updates, but all the eco-conscious information is above my pay grade." She gave a self-deprecating laugh. "Anyway, my priority today is getting your approval on the wine cellar. The Beverage Director tasks are running smoothly at Pacific Jewel Inn and on track for our hotel. My PnL projections for all the hotel budgets are lining up. I need as much time to study as possible."

"One more reason you need your own space. And, of course, we can hit the wine cellar first." And he needed some space to get this unwelcome need to clasp her gorgeous face in his hands and see if she tasted as good as she looked under control.

"Thanks. We're both going to be working around the

clock for a New Year's Eve opening, so where we sleep shouldn't be a big deal."

He ground his molars together. Her uttering the words "we sleep" in that sexy voice of hers was too much. His usual self-control was unraveling around her. Thank god she still saw him as a big brother.

Which was a good thing.

Wasn't it?

Fortunately, the turn-off was just ahead, and he flicked on his blinker. "Don't worry. Everything will be on schedule." He'd make sure of it.

Campbell leaned forward to admire the curving road, shrouded in trees with dappled rays of sunlight peeking through. "Gosh, the beauty of this place gets me every time. And there's a deer."

He braked––the road was deserted on an early Monday afternoon. Together they admired the graceful animal who stared at them with wide eyes before turning and casually melting off into the lush greenery. "We are in a different world, aren't we?"

She angled her gaze at him, her wide mouth curving up. "Will you be able to handle living in the country? It's definitely a simpler life than what either of us are accustomed to. But I'm excited to get away from the chaos of the San Fran restaurant scene."

He shrugged and stepped on the gas. "I'm ready to set down roots and live in a quieter place." For the first time in his life.

She tilted her head. "You've definitely moved around a lot. Is this the first time you've really wanted to stay somewhere long-term?"

He considered her question. "Yeah. This is the first place that feels like it could be home. Ryan offered me a choice and I had zero doubts. The last decade was about gathering the experience to launch our string of hotels and for me that meant checking out new places. And it's not like there isn't an airport or access to bigger cities if I want to travel."

"True. There's something magical here. And for me, being based in wine country for now makes the most sense."

"For now? I thought you planned on being based here?"' His gut tightened.

She sank back into the leather upholstery and looked out the passenger window. "Maybe."

"Maybe?"

She gave a dismissive wave of her hand. "Well, yeah. That's my plan for now. But once I achieve my Master Sommelier status next year, that might change."

He frowned. "Didn't you commit to opening all the hotels as Beverage Director? I thought that was your end goal?" Hotel Kings planned on opening five luxury boutique hotels throughout California within two years and the Paso location was only the second.

Her tone was casual. "I'm on board through next year for Monterey, Palm Springs, and Beverly Hills. You know that. But other opportunities to learn and grow could arise, like a Michelin Star restaurant in Europe. I don't want to decide my entire future this moment."

The muscles in the back of Jack's neck clenched, an unfamiliar frisson of tension sparking down his spine. He should be excited for her career goals but right now, not so much. "I guess I figured being Beverage Director for a string of 5-Star hotels would be enough."

She turned toward him, her arctic blue eyes cool. "For now. And maybe forever. The point is I don't know yet. Why is it such a big deal? I've worked my ass off to achieve this. It's not like I can't train Austin to step in or hire somebody else if, and big emphasis on if, I receive an offer I can't refuse.

Right now, all that matters is opening the hotels and passing my exams."

He turned down the tree-lined gravel road. "Sorry. Today has thrown me. We're here so let's focus on this meeting." She was right--it was her decision how to navigate her career. He'd store his reaction in the back of his brain to analyze later.

After a few minutes rattling along the uneven lane, she asked, "Will we pave the road or leave it gravel?"

His shoulders relaxed. "Ryan thinks leave it and I agree. Just to give it more of that old world feeling. We want the guests to feel like they're stepping off the grid."

Campbell nodded. "It helps that cell service is terrible out here. I imagine some of the guests will balk at that initially. Hopefully, they'll be able to settle in and focus on the deluxe amenities, natural beauty, and spectacular wine and food."

And they were back on easy footing again, where they needed to remain. "Well, it's clear in our marketing materials our hotel is unique--it won't be a surprise. And we're catering to a niche market."

"Yeah, but you know how things can go when they are in theory vs. reality. I'm confident with what we're planning for the restaurant and wine lounge the guests will never want to leave and will have booked a spot next year before they exit the property."

"I like your enthusiasm." He rounded the final bend and the world expanded, or at least that's how it felt each time he pulled up to the property.

His breath lodged in his throat. Wheat colored hills rolled out toward the horizon, with old oak trees and orchards spearing up in green splendor. Wild lilac framed the driveway up to the sprawling main building of what would soon be one of California's premiere boutique hotels. Once the bulldozers and orange cones and spider webs of gray scaffolding came down—the melding of the land's natural gifts with the best sustainability possible would be worth every hour of work and every cent. It would be fucking glorious.

Just like Ryan Michaels put his imprint on Pacific Jewel Inn, Maison du Soleil would bear Jack Cassidy's stamp. Finally, the man with shallow roots would test the depth of his desire to plant himself. He parked the SUV.

"Wow, they've made so much progress since I was here last week." Campbell clapped her hands together. "It makes it all seem more real, doesn't it?"

"Definitely. This walk-through should help shape up how the next month will go. Let's go check in with Brian for an overall update and then hit the wine cellar."

Together they crossed the rugged terrain, soon to become a smooth stone pathway leading to the hotel's entrance. Although the property was peaceful, the noise from buzz saws, hammering, and shouts from the crew left no doubt it was a work in progress. Sawdust drifted in the warm air, the scents of construction, and a hint of lilac surrounded them.

"Hey Campbell, Jack." A tall muscular man with a battered hard-hat called from across the broad expanse that would be the resort's front patio area.

Campbell touched Jack's arm, sending a shot of electricity through him. "Let's do this." Damn, he was in trouble if every brush of her fingers set him on high alert.

When they reached the foreman, his face lit up and he tipped his hat. "Great to see you again, Campbell."

"Hi Brian, nice to see you, too." Campbell flashed her gorgeous smile.

Jack grimaced. Did she find the guy attractive? Sure, he was blond and buff and wore a low-slung toolbelt, but that wasn't Campbell's type, was it?

Brian didn't even glance at Jack. "So do you guys want to

check on the exterior and see what's happening with the roofing prep for the solar panels or did you want to start somewhere else?"

Campbell shook her head. "Jack's going solo on all the exterior stuff a little later and my time is limited today. Do you mind if we go inside and see how the wine cellar is coming along?"

Brian's lean cheeks creased into a grin. "Anything for you. You're going to love the brick work. Come on, let's grab you both hard hats."

"You're the best." She started toward the entrance with Brian, leaving Jack to trail behind like he didn't exist. *What the hell?*

He caught up with them at the enormous open rectangle where glass doors would welcome in guests and grabbed the hard hat. Brian had already handed Campbell hers.

"Watch where you step. There's a lot going on today." Brian smiled down at Campbell.

Jack resolved to extinguish the flare of annoyance and focus on the building progress.

A combination of open air and enclosed spaces, the hotel would emphasize indoor/outdoor living while conserving energy. Jack couldn't wait to see the wrought iron benches and café tables, spots where guests could savor fresh air and sip wine from the world-class collection Campbell would curate. Peaceful, elegant, and luxurious.

They reached the broad arched doorway leading into the dark coolness of the future official wine cellar. Large temporary florescent lighting was set up around the otherwise empty windowless room. Tarps covered the rough surface beneath their feet, which would boast wide-planked oak floors.

Campbell twirled around the space, her hands clasped to

her chest. "Oh my god, it's perfect. Exactly like I envisioned it."

"Really?" It looked like an underground cavern to Jack.

She spun toward him, her pale skin gleaming beneath the artificial lights. "Absolutely. Look at the exposed brick along the back wall. It was repurposed from a giant outdoor fireplace and cleaned. And the wood for the wine cabinets and racks will cover the remaining walls and contrast perfectly with the oak floors. Wine will be showcased in glass cases and there will be French oak barrels in the corner. An enormous chandelier, with LED or halogen lighting of course, will be the centerpiece here." She pointed up to the unfinished ceiling.

Her enthusiasm was infectious. No way would he admit all he saw was a big, dark room. "So, you're happy with it?"

She vibrated with energy. "Yes I am. And it is naturally cool, which is what I was worried about when I learned we couldn't go underground. Again, that will help keep the wine the perfect temperature and humidity."

"And don't forget we're using solar power, so even during the hotter months, it will still be efficient to keep it cool in here," Brian said.

"Thank you so much. You are a magician." She beamed at the lead contractor.

"I don't know about that, but we wanted to make it exactly how you described it. Anything else you want to see?" Even in the florescent glare from the temporary lights, a flush stained the man's cheeks.

Campbell was truly irresistible when she focused her attention on someone. Her inner fire lit up the vast space and warmed anyone who was lucky enough to be in her sights. And apparently Brian was feeling lucky. Jack blew out an exhale.

"No, as long as we're on track to have it done in plenty of

time for the opening, I'm good. Jack?" She turned back to him, her delicate features alight with joy.

"You're the expert with all things wine, so if you're happy, I'm happy." He gave her a thumbs up.

Brian cleared his throat and finally looked at Jack. "Great, if we're done in here, let's go check on the rest of the renovations and we can discuss priorities over the next month, deal?"

Brian led them out of the wine room and along the corridor toward the east wing, where some of the deluxe suites would be located. Although the conversation shifted to organic gardens for the planned farm to table restaurant, Jack listened with only half an ear.

He forced himself to keep his gaze scanning the property and off the sway of Campbell's hips as she walked ahead of him with the contractor. Being laser-focused on work and filtering out distractions was one of his superpowers. Every minute in her presence weakened his resolve and fortified his desire for her. Somehow the woman was like his own personal kryptonite.

If he needed to pitch a damn tent at the hotel to avoid sharing an eight-hundred square foot apartment with her, so be it.

CHAPTER 3

Campbell collapsed onto the velvet sofa with a groan. Jack had dropped her at home and sped off to run errands. Or more likely, strong arm someone into giving him a place to stay. The man didn't often take no for an answer and if anyone could conjure an apartment out of thin air during 100% occupancy in wine country, it was Jack Cassidy.

Her teenaged daydreams didn't hold a candle to the reality of Mr. Thirst Trap Cassidy––the most handsome man in the universe. At least he'd seemed to have bought her act that she considered him a big brother. If this Master Sommelier gig didn't work out, she'd do great in theater––her acting skills were top notch.

Her phone chimed with her study-session reminder and now she groaned in earnest. If she didn't need two-inch thick reading glasses soon, it would be a miracle. *This is my dream. This is my dream. I want to do this more than anything in the world.* She parroted her mantra.

Her passion for wine fueled her dedication to her profession but memorizing types of soil was not fascinating. It couldn't all be glitz and glamour. Not that she wasn't committed to putting in the hours to achieve the highest echelon in her chosen field, but sometimes the rigorous requirements got to her.

Wine hadn't exactly been on her radar growing up in the Taylor household. Her parents were educators, which meant the household budget was tight. They'd lived in a modest ranch house and wine was usually reserved to celebrate special occasions.

It wasn't until she'd worked as an au pair during her year abroad studying at La Sorbonne that she'd been introduced to wine as an experience, a way of life, a ritualistic celebration. She'd taken care of twin five-year-old girls, Martine and Marlene Cocteau, for their diplomat father and socialite mother. One evening, Madame Cocteau had asked her to assist the staff for a special dinner party.

The guests had oohed and aahed over different vintages served with each of the five-course gourmet meal. Immediately intrigued, she started learning about wine, even traveling South to Bordeaux and Burgundy and the Rhône Valley. Rhône blends were her favorites, which was part of why Paso Robles wineries appealed to her. One more reason she loved this beautiful slice of the world where the ocean met the golden mountains.

Time to get off her butt and fill her emerald green leather messenger bag with her color-coded flashcards and meticulous notebooks. Everything was stored neatly in her desk/shelf combination, and she slipped what she needed into the roomy bag. To ensure a six-foot something distraction didn't arrive home before she'd completed her three hours of study time, she'd hit the library. Yeah, he was correct that the living situation wasn't ideal.

Her belly jumped. What had she done? The temptation of Jack was formidable, and she'd have to make sure she didn't succumb. No way could she survive the humiliation if he discovered her forever crush and laughed at or rejected her.

And now they were not just working together, they were sharing a confined space with only one bedroom. She snapped the bronze metal clasp shut and hoisted the bag over one shoulder.

It would be fine. Absolutely fine.

~

FOUR HOURS LATER, Campbell parked next to Jack's Range Rover and exhaled a steadying breath. As she suspected, he'd attempted to find his own place, to no avail. He'd texted her to let her know he'd beat her back to the condo.

The delicious aroma of mezcal brown sugar butter had tantalized her on the drive home and she couldn't wait to dig into the halibut dish. She'd offered to pick up dinner from one of her favorite spots, Fish Gaucho, as a "welcome to town/peace offering for giving away your apartment" meal. A bottle of her favorite French Chablis was chilling in the kitchen's small but state of the art wine fridge. By the time they ate the crème brûlée from a local brasserie to satisfy Jack's sweet tooth, he had to forgive her.

She unlocked the front door, crossed to the kitchen island, and placed the take-out bag onto the white quartz countertop. The only sound breaking the silence in the empty room was the whoosh of the shower. A visual of Jack's lean muscular frame covered with only droplets of hot water flashed before her eyes. Heat flared in her center.

Shaking the tempting vision from her traitorous brain, she busied herself arranging the food onto cheerful blue and yellow patterned plates. Maybe Jack was right to be so freaked out about their shared living arrangement because he sensed she was ready to pounce.

Methodical tasks were an excellent way to squash an over-active libido, right? She uncorked the bottle of wine and turned to pull down two glasses from a white farmhouse style cabinet.

The bathroom door flew open and there stood Jack, a white towel slung low around his narrow hips. His sleek skin gleamed with moisture from the shower, every sculpted inch of him from his broad chest down to his six-pack to the magical V-shaped grooves, absolutely flawless.

Her mind blanked. A shiver danced down her spine and the hairs on the back of her neck prickled. In college, she'd seen the statue of David on a weekend trip to Florence. She'd believed no mortal man could match Michelangelo's master-piece, but Jack could give the 17-foot-high marble sculpture real competition. *Damn.*

His crystal green eyes widened but he froze, framed in the doorway in all his masculine perfection. "Campbell, I didn't hear you come in."

She swallowed and licked her lips. "Umm…yeah, I just got home. I picked up dinner and opened up some wine and you should probably get dressed." Crap, had she said that out loud?

He glanced down and muttered something under his breath. "Sorry. I'm not used to anybody being around. Let me grab some sweats."

He pivoted and strode to the bedroom, the damp terry cloth not disguising an inch of his perfect round ass. Campbell's breath whooshed out and her legs trembled as she grabbed and guzzled crisp Chablis. Sometimes wine was meant to be studied and savored and other times it was more suited to soothe jangled nerves. A little grape fortification after he'd blown her fantasies out of the water.

She refilled the glass and circled around the bar to her stool. Time to act casual, like seeing Jack wearing only a towel hadn't affected her. Like it was no big deal. Half-naked gods paraded around her house all the time. She snorted and took another sip of wine.

Jack returned, wearing low slung gray sweatpants––was he kidding with this? Was he trying to kill her? Tempt her to pounce on him or what? He tugged down a faded black and red SDSU t-shirt but not before she'd drunk in another gulp of those washboard abs.

This is the price she paid for not having gone on a date in the last several months. She was sexually deprived, and he was there. That's all.

He joined her at the counter, the scent of soap and shampoo and clean laundry greeting her. "Thanks for picking up dinner. I'm starving." His voice was subdued.

An awkward silence hung over the room, the clicking of the silverware on ceramic the only relief from the unspoken tension. Her pulse hammered in her throat––she couldn't handle it. "So how did everything go this afternoon?"

Jack set down his fork and finally looked at her, his jaw tight, his eyes unreadable. "You're right. There is nowhere to stay within twenty-five miles, and I can't commute that far. So…" He shrugged and sipped his wine.

Time to return them to stable footing. Humor was her go-to. "So, you're admitting that I was right and you were wrong?" She flashed a toothy grin.

His severe expression relaxed, and he chuckled. "I admit nothing. I still wish I'd been able to negotiate with the land-lord and help him find a different option, but it is what it is."

"Exactly. I was right." She saluted him with her glass. "How delicious is this halibut?" The flaky white fish was perfectly prepared, with the appropriate amount of season-ing. Jack loved excellent food as much as she did.

He clinked his glass against hers, the muscles in his powerful forearm flexing. "You were definitely right about the fish. And I appreciate not having to think about groceries or anything tonight. It's been a long day."

"Well, I know our schedules are both super hectic and we probably won't see each other every night, so I figured I'd treat to welcome you to town." And squelch the sliver of guilt she couldn't shake off. But how could she have turned Kyle's sick father away?

"About that. How's that going to work with me sleeping out here and the dresser in the bedroom? I can't exactly barge into the room if I get back later than you." A crease appeared between his dark eyebrows.

She sighed. It was awkward. Even if she had looked at him like a brother—and that ship had sailed in high school—sharing the space with another person wasn't going to be easy. Add in the attraction factor and the damn gray sweatpants and she was in trouble.

"Why don't you leave most of your clothes in the bedroom and keep your pajamas—"

"Pajamas?" The dimple in his right cheek deepened before he burst out laughing.

"What's so funny?"

He shook his head. "I left my Star Wars footie pajamas in storage, so I guess I'll have to improvise."

She waved a hand. "Surely you have something to sleep in?" She'd buy him a head-to-toe flannel onesie to cover all that smooth skin.

"Well, I've lived alone for over a decade, so no, I don't have pajamas. Will boxers work?" His leaf-green eyes lit with mischief.

"And a t-shirt. Boxers and a t-shirt." No way would she survive seeing that carved torso on the regular. And please god let them be baggy boxers, not those snug boxer briefs.

He smirked. "Maybe. It's basically summer up here,

Campbell. I'm not going to sweat to death. You'll be in the other room anyway. So, does this mean you wear pajamas?"

She sniffed. "We do have air-conditioning, as you may have noticed. And of course I have pajamas. What if there was a fire in the middle of the night and I had to run outside? I like to be prepared."

No need for him to know she slept in an ancient tank-top and teeny boxers. Although maybe she should invest in that flannel onesie for herself. Another layer of defense against his proximity.

He chuckled again. "The things you think about. But yes, fair point. I'll tuck my boxers and t-shirt up in my bed-in-the-wall. It's almost like being back in boot camp."

Her lips twitched. "I remember Cam coming home after your summer ROTC programs in college and he would complain about trying to sleep in a bunk bed with big snoring hairy guys. At least we aren't in bunk beds, right?" Would he prefer top or bottom?

She crossed her legs and sucked in a deep breath. Time to drag her mind out of the gutter. Or the bed, as the case may be.

His gaze raked over her, his eyes heating. "You're definitely not a big hairy guy. I guess I'll find out if you snore if the walls start vibrating."

"Hey, right back at you. Anyway, because I did feel a little bad, I got dessert at BL Brasserie." She popped up off her seat, crossed to the refrigerator, and pulled out the crème brûlée.

"Crème brûlée? You're forgiven." He beamed like a little boy getting his favorite birthday cake.

"I thought it would do the trick. I know how much you loved it when my dad made it. We're sharing, though, because I love it, too." She dug two spoons out of the utensil drawer.

She set it down and refilled both of their glasses. Tonight called for finishing the bottle. Plus, it complemented the dessert.

He tapped on the burnt caramel, cracking it and scooped out some of the creamy custard. His eyes closed and he moaned. "That's amazing. Doesn't match Clyde Taylor's, but pretty close."

His guttural sound shot sparks straight down to her center. What noises did he make during sex? She scooted her stool away a few inches and reached for a bite, careful not to brush his long blunt fingers.

"Yeah, I discovered it my first week in town. Don't tell my dad." She set down her spoon. "So, I think we should set a few ground rules, so this living situation goes as smoothly as possible."

He sat up taller, one brow arched. "There's more than the pajamas? Are you assigning me dishes or trash duty? Like that chalkboard your mom kept in the kitchen listing out all your weekly chores."

She giggled. "That's an excellent idea. And you're responsible for both. What I actually meant was more along the lines of schedules and space. I think we need to be smart about it, so it doesn't affect either of our work."

"Only if I get an allowance." He laughed. "You're right. If I can have part of the desk and a drawer to leave some stuff, that will work. I can handle calls and some of the admin work at a coffee shop, so you'll have peace and quiet here. Do you have some hours in mind?"

"Well, that's the thing. It depends on the day. Most nights I'll need to hit the books and I can do that in the bedroom if you want to watch TV or whatever."

He nodded. "Okay. But I'm serious. If you need the place to yourself, tell me. I can make myself scarce. There's also some makeshift space at the hotel I can use. At some point, I need to set up an office over there."

"But with the construction, it's so loud from dawn to dusk. I know, I've been out there several times." She nibbled on her lower lip.

His gaze dropped to her mouth and his eyes narrowed. He quickly looked away, cleared his throat, and reached for his wine. "I know. But what do you do? Ryan did it in La Jolla. That's what those silencing earphones are for, right?"

The awkwardness evaporated and simmering awareness replaced it. "Yeah, I have them, too. Okay."

She paused and then figured why not get it all on the table. "I think as long as we can hold off the rest of the team coming up, nobody should find out about the apartment. As soon as harvest is done, you'll easily be able to move into another place. Can you make sure Cam doesn't pop down from Monterey?" Which was less than a two-hour drive.

"Yeah, he's really busy with renovations so that shouldn't be a problem. And harvest should be done by early to mid-October?"

Her shoulders softened. "Most places, yes. So, we're good until early October when I've tentatively coordinated a wine tasting dinner and meeting with Jordan Fiorentini and her crew at Epoch Winery. She offered up the owners' house for Ryan and the team to stay over that night. I really want to start a partnership with them––monthly wine dinner pairings or talks or education or really whatever the heck she'd want to do with us."

"That sounds incredible. And great idea to tie their visit to an event like that." He scrubbed his hands across his cropped dark hair. "And I'm wiped out. I may pull out my bed and read for a little bit. Is that cool with you?"

They'd always shared a love of books, although he favored gristly murder mysteries and romance was more her jam. "Of course. I was going to log a few more hours studying and can do that in my room."

"Let me do my first chore and clean up. Thanks again for getting dinner."

They both stood and Campbell stumbled into him. Jack caught her shoulders in his large hands and her fingers splayed across his powerful hard chest.

She tilted her head back and their gazes locked. "Jack." His name escaped on a long breathy sigh. Every inch of her was pressed against his chiseled body and a shiver rushed through her.

His eyes hooded and he yanked her closer. He slid his hands up to frame her face and lowered his mouth to hers in a whisper of a kiss. Sampling. Testing. Asking.

She answered. Her lips parted and their tongues tangled and stroked and sparred. He tasted like crème brûlée and heaven and how she'd always imagined his beautiful mouth would feel against hers. She slid her arms around his neck, thrusting her fingers into his close-cropped dark hair. A hum escaped her throat and she changed the angle of the kiss, teasing and tasting.

She dug her nails into his scalp. *More.* She wanted more of him. Needed more. His clean masculine scent, his powerful body, the overwhelming sense of him, was like a match tossed onto the fire raging inside her.

He growled, stroked his hands down her back, and cupped her ass, rocking her against the steel ridge of his arousal. He slanted his mouth across hers and took her deeper. The overhead lights and the rest of the world receded and all her focus narrowed down to their connection.

The heat blazed between them.

He pulled his head back, his breath ragged, his eyes closed, the dark lashes fanning out over his cheekbones. He lowered his head again and trailed kisses down her neck and found the tender spot in the hollow of her throat. Goose-bumps erupted along her skin and her back arched, crushing her breasts against him. Her head lolled back, suddenly too heavy to handle the onslaught of sensation coursing through her.

"Campbell," he rasped her name and the hint of stubble on his jaw felt like a rough cat's tongue against her skin.

She shivered. "Jack." She kept her eyes squeezed shut, unwilling to allow anything to invade this perfect bubble enveloping them.

A sharp chime sounded from a distance, piercing said bubble. For a moment, neither of them moved.

"That's not my phone." Jack clasped her shoulders and set her away from him.

Without the support of his muscular frame, her legs wobbled, and she gripped the back of the stool to steady herself. The phone continued to play its invasive tune. She really needed to change that ringtone. She shook her head, trying to orient herself.

"You going to answer it?" Jack's voice came from across the room now. He'd created distance between them.

She glanced down at the counter and cursed under her breath. Her brother. Talk about timing. Terrible timing. Did he have a sixth sense or something? The ringing stopped and she exhaled a shaky breath. She could call Cameron back in the morning. The situation here in the apartment needed her attention more.

Jack stood with his back to her, one hand braced against the wall, the other gripping the back of his neck.

Was he already regretting their kiss?

CHAPTER 4

$\mathcal{J}$ack couldn't face Campbell yet––he was furious with himself. Damn it, not even twenty-four hours and he'd blown his self-control. What kind of asshole was he? He ground his molars together and worked to slow the slamming of his heart against his ribs.

And if his best fucking friend hadn't called? He'd been on the verge of boosting Campbell onto the kitchen island and, with her passionate responsiveness, they wouldn't have stopped until they'd both come apart.

Jack flinched when the phone started ringing again. His limbs were heavy, like the feeling when you can't outrun the zombie in a nightmare. He turned back toward her.

Campbell held up the phone and her brother's name flashed on the screen, like one of those late-night billboards or the glare of police lights pulling you over for speeding.

Not that Jack was feeling guilty or barreling out of control or anything.

She cleared her throat, her voice husky and raw. "It's Cam again. I've got to take it."

Jack's gut clenched. Cam had never been the most talkative guy, but since he'd returned from Afghanistan after losing the lower half of his left leg, he'd grown almost taciturn. It wasn't like her brother to call repeatedly.

She smoothed back her golden hair and answered. "Hey Cam, what's up?" She sounded poised and calm.

"Dad? No, I haven't talked to him today." Her voice rose two octaves. "An accident?" The color drained from her cheeks, and she sank onto a barstool.

Jack pivoted and crossed the room in two strides. His throat tightened––the Taylors were family.

She held up a hand. "I'll call Dad now. Don't worry, he would have told you if it was serious. You said Camille's picking them up in half an hour. I'll call her and get the full scoop."

Campbell ended the call and carefully placed the phone on the countertop. She leaned back in the stool and scrubbed her face with her hands.

"What happened? Do we need to go up to San Francisco? Tell me what I can do." He squeezed her slender shoulder.

She relaxed into his touch and gazed up at him, her blue eyes damp. "Some stupid drunk driver rear-ended my parents and totaled their Buick. My dad called Cam to say they were fine, but mom's getting treated for minor injuries, whatever that means. My sister's there, thank god. They have to be okay, right?"

Jack gave a reassuring nod. "If your sister is picking them up so soon, that's a good sign. Otherwise, the doctors would keep them for observation." Not that he was an expert on it, but he'd handled a few car accident cases for friends over the years.

"Good point, but remember when I hit black ice and totaled that rental car in Canada five years ago? I walked away, thought I was fine and then boom, two weeks later I couldn't get out of bed. Now I've got back issues."

He frowned. "I think I was living in New York or maybe it was Atlanta, and you mentioned an accident, but I didn't know you were still dealing with back pain. I'm sorry, Campbell, that's tough."

She waved a hand, snatched up her phone, and tapped out a message. "I never really talked about it, and I keep it under control. Give me a few minutes, I'm going to text my dad."

Jack cleared the dishes and set them in the sink. He flipped on the faucet, squirted some deep-cleaning detergent, and filled the sink with bubbles. He might as well be useful because for once in his life he didn't have a quick reply or solution.

Moving quickly and deciding without prevaricating were part of his DNA. Perfect for business negotiations but not so much with impulse control, at least with Campbell. All those qualities had merged into one terrible decision: kissing his best friend's little sister––his co-worker and roommate.

Damn, the temptation was all too much. Sharing dinner, listening to her melodic voice, admiring her drive and talent, and being enveloped in her floral scent had simply caused his brain to flip off and instinct to take over.

The minute he'd caressed her soft curves, he hadn't been able to resist discovering if she tasted as delicious as she felt. And when he'd hesitated, giving her the chance to say no, she'd parted those sweet pink lips for him and offered him a sample of heaven.

He grabbed the sponge, plunged his hands into the water, then yelped and jumped back. He hadn't noticed the steam or the fact he'd only turned on the hot water. Talk about unnecessary symbolism. He bit off a curse.

"You okay over there?"

"I'm fine. Water is too hot." His hands tightened on the silverware, and he angled his head toward her.

She approached and brushed his shoulder. "Jack."

The color had returned to her high cheekbones, but a crease formed between her brows. "My dad hasn't returned my message yet. I'm worried."

"Oh, sweetheart." He dropped the fork, shook off the water, and turned to wrap her in a bear hug.

She pressed her cheek against him and slid her arms around his waist. He rested his chin on her soft hair. "Your parents are going to be fine."

"But what if the accident had been worse? What if one of them had been killed or seriously hurt? I can't lose my parents––they are the two best people I know. They don't deserve this." She mumbled the words against his chest, and he sucked in a sharp inhale.

He massaged between her shoulder blades, wanting to wipe the worry from her heart. "But they *are* fine." He hoped.

"You're probably right. But it's another reminder that we don't know what's around the corner. I'll never forget getting the call about Cam getting injured. His life will never be the same." She tilted her head back and looked up at him.

He brushed away the single tear clinging to her long eyelashes. "What happened to Cam sucks, but all he ever wanted was the military and he'd do it again. We can't live life in fear of what might happen."

Her lips curved up in a watery smile. "Thanks for talking me off the wall. Today has been…a lot."

He grimaced and stepped back, away from the heat of her. "Yeah. About that. Look, I'm sorry about what happened tonight. It won't happen again."

Her cerulean eyes widened. "You're sorry?"

He nodded. "Well, yeah. I shouldn't have taken advantage of you, and it won't happen again."

She rolled her eyes. "Taken advantage of me? Come on, I'm not some blushing virgin dallying with you in the gardens at a Regency Ball. It was just a kiss. It's not a big deal."

Was she really this nonchalant? "It's more complicated than that and you know it. We've both got priorities and they're already compromised with sharing a one-bedroom apartment and working together. The last thing we need is for the team to think we're hooking up." His friends would be beyond disappointed.

She crossed her arms over her chest and arched one eyebrow. "Well, I can handle it and I'm sure if I wasn't Cam's little sister, you wouldn't feel the need to apologize. Don't worry, our secret is safe with me."

"Look, Campbell, you've always been like a little sister to me. And now you've grown up into a brilliant, beautiful woman that no man with a pulse could resist. But it was a mistake, and it can't happen again. We've already agreed that opening the hotel and you passing your next exam are what matters. We can't muddy the waters with..." He blew out a breath.

Her lips drew into a tight line. "Fine. I get it. You're a man with a pulse and you like kissing beautiful women, I was just handy. And thanks for the reminder that I need to study. I'll do that in my room." She pivoted away.

He gritted his teeth––now he sounded like a total jerk. But maybe it was better if she believed he wasn't attracted to her. Safer anyway.

Her phone vibrated on the counter and this time her dad's name popped up.

He waited. Needed to know that Clyde and Christine were indeed fine.

She read the message and sighed, her shoulders softening. She met his gaze. "Camille picked them up and they are on their way home. Just some bumps and bruises, and my mom has a sprained wrist."

His jaw relaxed and he smiled. "That's great news."

"Of course. I know you love them, too. Good night." She turned and marched to her bedroom, pulling the door shut with a decisive click.

Pinned to the spot, he stared at the door. How the hell had today even happened? This attraction to Campbell had to be buried deep in the vault, so deep it didn't have a chance of resurgence. He'd focus on work and do what he'd done since law school--keep relationships light, straightforward with clear parameters, and zero expectations.

Campbell did not fit in that category.

Sure, they would see each other at the hotel, but there would always be other people around. He'd make damn sure they weren't alone together in the apartment.

For his own sanity. Because the idea of her sleeping with only a thin wall between them was enough to make him lose control all over again.

CHAPTER 5

Campbell smacked her alarm clock, the old-fashioned dial proclaiming it was minutes before 7 a.m. The apartment was silent. Part of her wanted to tip-toe to the door and peek out to see if Jack was snoozing wearing only a pair of boxers. Not that she was a voyeur or anything.

She huffed out a breath and replayed the prior night. Had he really bumbled through a non-apology claiming any guy would kiss her? Taking out any personal attraction from the equation? She reached up and pressed her fingers to her lips, still swollen from Jack's kisses. Which felt very personal, thank you very much. The chemistry between them had snapped and crackled like those 4th of July twizzle sparklers.

For years, she'd measured her attraction to other guys on what she secretly called the "Jack scale." After kissing him, she could confirm that not one of those men could compare. Last night probably shouldn't have happened, but now she knew. Jack's chiseled mouth had offered her the best kiss of her life, like she'd always imagined.

Nobody ever lived up to the sheer male beauty. The charismatic irresistible personality. The whip-smart brain.

But last night's stiff, formal apology? Completely out of character. Did it mean he'd been as blown away as she was or was that wishful thinking? On that note, what did she want from him? She squeezed her eyes shut.

But first, time to stretch. Ever since she'd been in that dumb accident in Calgary, her lower back troubled her. On the days when she failed to perform her lower body stretches and supine twists, the tight muscles would scream at her. For someone who'd been an elite collegiate soccer player, it was especially frustrating. Her days of sprints and high-impact soccer drills were now distant memories.

She hugged her right knee in, pressed it across her body and dropped her head toward her right arm. Now that she spent hours sitting and studying instead of being immersed in the hectic rhythm of restaurant life, she had to schedule in more physical activity. If she got up and moved around every hour while she was hitting the books or even attending tastings, she could keep her spine relatively pain-free.

She unwound to center and repeated the move on the other side before rolling out of bed.

Refreshed, she sauntered to the door, cracked it open, and sniffed the fragrant air appreciatively. The heavenly scent of French Roast coffee greeted her nostrils. She glanced down at her ancient, practically transparent ribbed tank and cotton shorts. God forbid she tempt the "just a man with a pulse" with her scanty attire.

She grabbed her short peacock blue robe that one of her girlfriends had brought her from a yoga retreat in Bali. Campbell had chosen a local wine seminar with a well-known expert from Bordeaux over the dreamy vacation. One day she'd travel more——it was one of the perks of up-leveling in her profession.

She belted the robe and ventured into the apartment. The Murphy Bed was once again part of the wall, and the space was deserted. Drawn in by the delicious aroma, she crossed to her fancy stainless-steel coffee maker--certain splurges were worth every penny. Her favorite "No coffee, no talk" mug sat on the counter next to a single sheet of paper. She snatched it up.

Headed to the property early. Brewed the coffee strong as tar, just how you like it. Don't wait up for me. –Jack

Her lips twitched. Yeah, she went through a phase after her semester in Paris where she turned her nose up at anything less potent than double espresso. After a few years of wildly fluctuating heartbeats and sleepless nights, she'd dialed it back to darker than dark, no sugar. Jack took his with four sugars and cream--she'd always teased him that he should have warm milk and cookies instead.

She poured her coffee and sipped--perfection. Maybe after she was fully caffeinated, she'd have an epiphany about Jack. The angel on her shoulder lectured her to focus on work, studying, and treating Jack like a family friend. The devil reminded her life was short and to remember how incredible being plastered against Jack's rock-hard body felt. Would it be so terrible to have a fling? What was one more secret when they were already keeping their living situation under wraps, right?

She huffed out a breath--if Jack and everyone they knew discovered she'd nursed a crush since high school, she'd feel like a fool. Time to get to work. She sauntered over to her desk and flipped open her favorite daily planner to skim her schedule. She had a few video calls, one with Austin about the chef candidates for Chez Paul Marc, and another with her Master Sommelier mentor, Xavier.

He'd set up a few tastings for them today, all aligned with her exam preparation. Even though the tastings were technical and designed to help her discern specific details, sampling wine was one of her favorite aspects of her career.

She finished her coffee and picked up her phone to check in on her parents.

Her dad picked up on the first ring. "We're fine, honey."

Her lips curved up at his light tone--her dad always downplayed anything negative. "Good morning to you, too. I've been worried. Are you sure you're okay? I can't believe your car was totaled--that's major."

"We're in better shape than the car, that's for sure. Please don't worry about us."

"Well, please take it easy because it hasn't even been twenty-four hours. Don't forget that I felt fine until almost two weeks after I hit that black ice. Did they x-ray your back and neck last night?"

"Okay, Dr. Taylor. They did take x-rays and they were normal--well normal for two old people. Your mom sprained her wrist but otherwise we're fine. We'll take it easy. Tell me how everything is going there. Isn't Jack arriving any day?"

Heat rose in her cheeks. "He actually got here yesterday, and we've already been out to the hotel. Everything is going well, just a bit hectic."

"Oh good. I'm glad you've got Jack there now. He's such a great kid and I know you were holding down the fort while everyone was working on opening Pacific Jewel Inn."

Campbell snorted. "Um, Jack is 35 now, not exactly a kid. Now he's here, we're kicking it into high gear. Once harvest is over, the rest of the team will come up to fill in the gaps."

He chuckled. "As long as I call you kids, I can stave off feeling like an old man for a while longer. How is your studying going?"

"Okay, you can call us all kids if it makes you feel better. But you'll never seem old to me." She beamed--she was an unabashed daddy's girl. "I won't fail the test a second time. I'm meeting with my mentor today, actually."

"I'm not worried except about your tendency to be too hard on yourself. I'm so proud of you." His deep voice lowered.

Her heart warmed. "I love you, Dad. I'm so lucky to have you. Is Mom around?"

"She's sleeping right now. She had a tough night with the splint on her arm, but she's fine. We'll see you soon. We've got some news we want to share in person."

"News?" Her parents were approaching retirement age, but both were so energetic, she couldn't imagine them slowing down.

He chuckled. "Like I said, we'll share in person. Nothing urgent. And I know you've got a lot on your plate, so I'll tell your mother you called. I love you."

"You too, Dad. Don't forget to take it easy, okay?"

After they hung up, she unrolled her yoga mat and secured her phone to the stand where she could stream her thirty-minute slice of sanity workout. It always helped clear her head and after last night, a little focus on breath and movement would be welcome. Maybe she'd get a bolt of clarity signaling how to act natural when she saw Jack again.

"No, we cannot substitute the French oak barrels we're planning on using for the internal doors and trim. I don't care what you need to do to make this happen but find them somewhere." Jack stalked around the perimeter of his car, keeping his voice level with Herculean effort.

Between the cacophony of construction racket and the crick in his neck from tossing and turning all night on the most uncomfortable bed he'd had the bad luck to get stuck with since ROTC boot camp, he was not in the mood for this crap.

Now the vendor was trying to tell him he could only deliver one-third of the promised shipment--which was already nine days late and counting.

Not today, Satan. Jack cut off the guy's litany of lame excuses. "Look, I'm going to hang up now. Fix it or there will be consequences, got it?" And now he sounded like a cheap TV movie mobster.

He powered down the phone and slid it into the back pocket of his jeans. Dark denim was yet another bad decision piled on top of the many he'd made in the last twenty-four hours. Even though York Mountain was supposed to be cooler than the rest of the area, Santa Ana winds had carried in scorching dry temperatures.

Usually, he wasn't an irritable guy and prided himself on his cool, savvy reputation.

Not so much today. In his defense, the prior day and evening would have tested anyone's limits. The week was not progressing according to schedule. Instead of making headway and working hard toward the opening of Maison du Soleil, he was basically couch surfing like a college kid.

If that wasn't bad enough, he'd kissed his best friend's little sister. Cam already gave him reams of shit for being a player and for changing jobs and cities every few years. Jack was determined to plant roots in Paso Robles and prove to everyone that he wasn't like his parents--he could stick to one place.

He wiped the sweat beading on his forehead. Campbell was too tempting. For years, she'd been Campbell the badass soccer player. Campbell the badass Valedictorian. Cam's baby sister. And ever since Hotel Kings LLC launched, he'd learned that Campbell Taylor was a badass talented, tempting woman.

Now that he'd tasted her, he was screwed.

Royally screwed.

He massaged the back of his neck and closed his eyes, blocking out the blinding sunshine for a moment. The kiss they'd shared had blown him away. She'd tasted sweet, like ripe berries and heaven. Her unique flavor still lingered--crowding his thoughts, weighing on his senses. And wasn't that dangerous?

A man's voice shouting his name forced him out of his contemplation. Brian--was the guy fantasizing about Campbell, too? He shook his head--no time to worry about that now.

He pivoted toward the hotel and strode to meet the foreman, who would be furious when he learned that Jack hadn't been able to negotiate an immediate solution.

Jack stopped and held up both hands. "Don't shoot the messenger. I hope to have good news by this afternoon about the delivery. For now, can you shift the focus elsewhere and come back to the doors?"

Brian frowned and shook his head. "Those materials were supposed to arrive last week. I'm already juggling things. We can do it, but it sure is a pain in the neck."

Jack's neck throbbed. "Yeah, a pain in the neck all the way around. Anything else I can do to make a difference?" As if his to-do list wasn't already a marathon he didn't care to race.

Brian cocked his head. "You got here before most of the guys already and I know you're plenty busy. But there are a few spaces we didn't get to yesterday. You up for coming out to the pool area with me? I've got a few landscaping suggestions that aren't included in the current plans."

If spending fifteen minutes checking out where they would have a gorgeous natural looking pool and spa water-fall would appease the contractor, it was worth it. Plus being outside and checking out his hotel never got old. A swell of pride filled his chest. Sure, this was one of the Hotel Kings' properties, but it was his baby. And he wanted the seeds he was planting to flourish and be the best.

They traversed broad, open walkways, picking across tarp covered floors and relatively neat stacks of hardware and supplies. The hotel was taking shape and if it turned out as designed, it would be breathtaking, unique, and earn them the Platinum LEED certification. The Paso Robles community valued the environmental initiatives, and the Hotel Kings were thrilled to create a property with state-of-the-art sustainability.

Epoch Winery, their neighbor and hopefully a partner in exclusive wine events, was a shining example of what an eco-conscious establishment could be. They'd resourced materials from the original York Mountain Winery to build their tasting room and Jack hoped to emulate their example. Besides, they consistently produced some of his favorite reds, like Epoch's masterpiece Syrah, Block B.

Time to redirect his focus to the dreams he and Ryan, Cam, Lucas, and Austin had been working toward for the last decade. He listened to his foreman and tucked Campbell into the back corner of his brain.

For now.

CHAPTER 6

Campbell let herself into the apartment and scanned the space for signs of life. It was 4:30 on Saturday afternoon, and she hadn't seen Jack since they'd kissed on Monday night. Somehow, he had managed to avoid her, returned after she was asleep, and left before she woke. Except for some work emails and a team conference call, they hadn't communicated.

Before dawn the other day, she'd thought she'd heard the shower and there were small signs--toothbrush, towel hanging on the rack, but he'd essentially morphed into the invisible man. Although he'd brewed her coffee every morning, he hadn't left another note.

It was rather insulting. Beyond rude. And frankly immature.

Had kissing her really freaked him out that much? Imagine if he'd had an inkling of her major crush?

He'd probably camp out at the hotel.

She huffed and marched to the refrigerator and poured herself a glass of iced green tea. If he actually stopped skulking in and out of the apartment, maybe they could establish some kind of normalcy. Surely, they could hang out for dinner or coffee here and there without ripping each other's clothes off. *Enough.*

She squared her shoulders and dug her phone out of her purse. She'd text him and demand they talk. Once they'd cleared the air, her usual razor-sharp focus would resume. Of course, he'd played the starring role in her distractions and daydreams this week. Time to change the channel.

Hey Jack, when will you be back? We need to talk, okay?

She strolled to the couch, sank into the velvet cushions, and sipped her drink. She dropped her phone next to her, turned on some streaming music––classic Foo Fighters to lift her mood––and resolved not to obsess when three little dots appeared or didn't appear.

The doorknob turned, and Jack appeared in the doorway, looking tall, lean, and a little rumpled in a smoke gray polo and dark jeans. "Let me get some water and we'll talk." His voice was husky.

He set his briefcase on the desk and crossed to the refrigerator. She waited until he sank into the armchair across from her. "Want me to start?"

He gestured with his glass and chugged half of it. "Sure."

She leaned back and crossed one leg, striving for nonchalance. "Look, this is ridiculous. You can't keep sneaking out before I wake up and coming back when I'm asleep."

He covered his eyes with a hand. "I know. I'm sorry. I'm exhausted." He peered at her between his fingers with puppy dog eyes.

She shook her head. "For god's sake, Jack. I don't get it. We're adults. We've known each other forever. You're acting like the boy who turned me down for the Sadie Hawkins dance in junior high and avoided my locker for the next six months. What's your deal?"

He choked on a sip of water and doubled over with

laughter. "A boy turned you down for the dance? Did Cam kick his ass for you?"

Heat rose in her cheeks. "It's not funny. I didn't tell anyone. I locked myself in my bedroom and listened to angsty rock on repeat." She hadn't even wanted to ask Jimmy Jarvis, but her girlfriends had bullied her into it. Even now, the embarrassment washed over her.

He shook his head. "Well, if that kid saw you now, he'd regret it. And I know I've been acting like an idiot. It's not you--"

She pointed a finger at him. "Oh no, don't give me that me and you nonsense. We're never going to survive the next month—you definitely aren't going to survive without sleep—if you don't stop. I promise your virtue is safe with me."

His lips twitched and he quirked one dark brow. "My virtue?"

"Well, I can't figure out why else you would avoid me like this." She folded her arms across her chest.

"I'm sorry. I thought some space would be a good idea for both of us. Can I take you to dinner tonight and we'll start over?" His jade-colored eyes pleaded with her.

Her heart skipped a beat. "Absolutely. A very expensive dinner and I get to order the wine. From a Reserve list. I've got a few connections, so I'm sure I can get us in."

"I look forward to taking advantage of those connections." He glanced down at his over-sized stainless-steel watch. "Should we try to get in soon?"

"Yes, it will be easier if we go eat with the early birds. Most visitors spend the day wine tasting and prefer later reservations on Saturdays." She tapped her finger against her lip, considering which spot she was in the mood for tonight.

"Okay if I crack that bottle of the 2018 Epoch white? I've been eyeing it since I got here."

"Oh, in the pre-dawn darkness?" She couldn't stop the snark.

"Hey smart-ass, I thought we had a truce." His handsome face spread into a beguiling grin, designed to snuff all resistance.

And his charm was irresistible. "Just teasing. You can still handle some good old-fashioned sarcasm, right?"

"Yeah." He winked.

"Let me send a few texts and see what magic I can work for us." She pulled up her contacts and shot off a few messages. Over the last few months, she'd been cultivating connections with local restaurant owners and staff. Excellent relationships would create not only reciprocal referrals but a sense of community.

Jack uncorked and poured two glasses of the straw-gold wine. He joined her on the couch, and she sniffed her wine appreciatively, the citrus zest and honeyed notes apparent on the nose.

Her phone pinged. "That was fast." She read the message on her phone and her jaw dropped. *Oh shit.*

Jack leaned forward and placed his glass on the coffee table. "Campbell? What's wrong?"

She tossed her phone on the plum-colored cushion and took a very un-sommelier like swig of her wine. Fortification was required to concoct a fast plan. One part of her registered the delicious flavors exploding on her tongue but the rest of her short-circuited.

His long, blunt fingers clasped her forearm. "Campbell, you're scaring me. Is it your parents? A complication from the accident?'

She exhaled a shaky breath. "No, no. They're fine. So fine, in fact, that they are going to be here in half an hour to take us out to dinner."

Jack reared back. "What? Here?"

Sweat prickled on the back of her neck and her breath hitched. "Yeah, here. My dad thought it would be lovely to surprise us because they have some big news. And my brother and sister are coming with them. They have reservations at 6 at Il Cortile."

"Shit. *Shit.* How are we going to do this? They'll ask about my place. They'll see my stuff here. Cam is going to flip out." Jack lunged to his feet and looked around wildly.

She'd never seen the smooth, answer-for-everything Jack Cassidy in such a state. Although, to be fair, her heart was hammering so hard it might jettison through her ribcage.

It wasn't like they were in a YA novel where the older brother was a Senior in high school and his buddy was hitting on his sophomore little sister. They were both in their thirties.

But her brother had grown more intense since returning from the Middle East, and her entire family knew both her and Jack too well. It would be tough enough to hide the simmering attraction between them in public. Neither of them needed questions about the apartment or more drama. He was absolutely correct.

She stood and glanced at the desk, looking for signs of Jack's occupancy. "Okay, stay calm. I'm going to text them and say we'll meet them at the restaurant. That we're out somewhere and it will be easier."

He nodded. "Yeah, that's smart."

She grabbed her phone and typed. Her dad pinged back his agreement.

"Okay. Phew." She literally wiped her brow like a shoplifter approaching the exit with a pilfered Fendi bag under her arm. "We need to change and get out of here. And put on your defense lawyer hat and formulate the perfect denial for them coming over here after dinner."

"Hey, I'm a contracts guy. Not a criminal attorney. But yeah, we'll come up with something."

They rushed toward the bedroom to change clothes. Campbell slowed before they bumped into each other. In her heightened state, brushing against Jack was dangerous. Time to put him in the friend zone.

"Let me grab clothes from the bedroom. If that's okay?" He hesitated, a flicker of worry flashing through his expressive eyes.

She nodded. "Of course." Not awkward at all. Not like she wanted to see him peel off that polo shirt and shuck his pants. Nope, not her.

"And make sure not to sit next to me, okay?" He called over his shoulder.

"Seriously? That's plain rude." Although it was probably wise. Even if her reserved older brother didn't notice the sparks crackling between them, her mom's eagle eye wouldn't miss it. And she would call Campbell out on it later, in private where Campbell wouldn't be able to evade her questions.

She entered the bathroom, locking the door behind her. The hammered silver framed mirror reflected her flushed cheeks and wild eyes. Oh god, being in proximity with Jack made her hot. Literally. And the rush of adrenaline over her family's surprise visit didn't help her nerves.

She shook her head. Time to at least *appear* like she was fine. Doing a quick assessment, she grabbed her navy eyeliner and drew on a quick cat eye, brushed some clear gel on her full eyebrows. No blush needed tonight. Her favorite pinky-nude lipstick was in her purse. A quick spritz of dry shampoo to her roots and she was good to go.

She whipped open the door and there was Jack, looking scorching hot in a white linen button-down that highlighted his broad shoulders and tapered to his narrow waist. Jeans hugged his long muscular legs. Her belly tightened and she sucked in a deep inhale. He smelled like clean laundry and a hint of pine––his scent as delicious as his appearance.

"Perfect timing." His straight white teeth flashed against his tawny skin. He seemed completely unruffled and calm, like they weren't about to go lie to her family for an evening.

She cleared her throat. "You look great. Give me a couple minutes to throw on a sundress and I'll be good to go." She hurried past him into her bedroom and closed the door. *Focus on acting natural tonight.*

She whipped open the closet door and stared at her clothes. The perennial question: what to wear? She had a carefully curated wardrobe. Her work as a sommelier—soon to be Master Sommelier—required she have chic outfits that weren't too sexy or too conservative. The focus was always on the wine, but she tried to emulate the Parisians, who managed a casual unstudied elegance.

She also had her "off-duty" dresses and she selected one of her favorites. A deep rose silk maxi dress with skinny straps and a deep double V-neck. Perfect for an awkward dinner with her family. Ugh, hopefully she was blowing it all out of proportion. It wasn't like her relatives were mind readers. If she and Jack could avoid the topic of where they were living, they would be good. Right?

CHAPTER 7

*J*ack gazed down at Campbell, resisting the urge to stroke the strands of silvery blonde hair spilling over her toned shoulders. Wearing a gorgeous dress that skimmed her slim, athletic build, she looked beyond tempting. Laughter, music, and the clink of cocktails filled the early evening air. Downtown Paso was in full Saturday night swing, with sidewalk cafes and restaurants buzzing with customers.

They turned the corner from Spring Street where they'd lucked into a parking spot, onto 12th Street, where they were meeting the Taylors at Il Cortile Ristorante. "Okay, if anyone asks questions about the apartment, I'll answer."

Campbell nodded. "As long as you make sure nobody tries to come over for a night cap, my lips are sealed."

"Let's just do our best not to screw up. And nobody is coming over."

"It's all a little cloak and dagger. Maybe we're being ridiculous. Kind of like you've been all week hiding out." She shook her hair back over her shoulders and a hint of her light floral scent reached him.

He blew out a breath. "Hey. There's a lot riding on the hotel opening and neither of us need complications." Why did he have to keep repeating that over and over?

"It will all be fine." A note of doubt crept into her usually confident voice. "Here we are."

The charming Italian restaurant boasted a modern cream-colored awning and a wrought iron fenced in patio. Jack spotted the Taylors and squared his shoulders, like he was heading into a major contract negotiation.

Or a dinner where he was going to lie to the people who had essentially taken him under their wing and treated him like a second son. The same set of honorary parents and best friend who trusted him implicitly and vice-versa. The same best friend who assumed Jack was as protective of his little sister as he was.

Jack gritted his teeth. It had only been a kiss, for fuck's sake. Maybe he was blowing it all out of proportion, like Campbell said. But damn, that kiss had launched a host of ice-cold showers and dates with his left hand. Beyond awkward. When had Campbell changed from a comfortable friend to a dangerous distraction?

As an attorney, he was used to playing his cards close to the vest. Of polishing his position and presenting the best side. It was part of why he'd chosen contract law instead of litigation, because it was essentially cut and dry. And he never veered into fabrication at work or in his personal life. His gut twisted because some sixth sense signaled that habit was about to be tested tonight.

"Jack. Campbell, over here." Christine Taylor waved from a corner table, a black splint covering her forearm and hand.

"Oh geez, look at her wrist," Campbell muttered under her breath and caught his arm, steering him toward the front door. "We have to go inside to the hostess stand and they'll escort us out."

He flinched and shifted a step away from her. Time to create the distance, starting now. "Got it."

They entered the restaurant and an elegant dark-haired man in formal black slacks and a crisp white shirt greeted them and led them to the table.

Christine and Clyde rose and rushed over to hug them, leaving Cam still seated. They were a handsome couple—it was easy to see where their children got their good looks.

Jack pulled Christine, or Mrs. T as he'd always called her, into a bear hug, careful to avoid her arm. She squeezed him right back. "It's been too long, Jack Cassidy. I'm so glad you're going to be in one place and close by, too."

Warmth filled him and he grinned down at her. "A three-and-a-half-hour drive isn't that close, but it's definitely better than a six-hour flight." Another reason he was happy to be settling in Paso Robles. Proximity to the Taylors.

Christine's delicate triangular face, so like her daughter's, softened with her lovely smile. "We'll be discussing that tonight. One of the reasons we were eager to come down and surprise you both."

They sat and as luck would have it, or not, Campbell sank into the chair between her parents, which left Jack to slide into the shallow booth next to his buddy. Cam lightly punched his shoulder and nodded. Always the effusive one, his friend.

"Where's Camille? I assumed she was driving you down?" Campbell looked between her parents.

Clyde shook his head. "No, she canceled at the last minute for a work event she had to attend with Sean. She said she'd call you later this week to catch up."

Campbell's shoulders softened and Jack read her mind. One less person to prevaricate in front of tonight. Now it was just her parents and her brother.

"I actually drove us down. Mom and Dad came to

Monterey to see the property and are staying with me tonight." Cam sipped his ice water, his voice controlled.

"How's everything going?" Jack angled toward his buddy. Keep the subject on the hotels and less personal tonight. Perfect.

Cam shrugged a shoulder. "It's a lot with all the different buildings, but renovations are under way and it's going to be really great."

The Monterey resort was the largest of the Hotel Kings' properties and would house upwards of one hundred and forty guests. It had been a small farm near the ocean and they were converting it into a variety of guest houses, to accommodate both large groups and individual guests. Each Hotel Kings' hotel was unique and would blend with the community in which it stood.

Mrs. T added, "We took a tour today and it's breathtaking. That's going to be the main wedding venue out of all the properties, right?"

Campbell nodded. "It is. Although technically we can hold weddings at any of the hotels, Cypress Coast Ranch is ideal. Charlie is hiring a wedding planner."

"If only one of my children would get married and give me grandbabies." Mrs. T gave an exaggerated sigh and scanned the table. "Camille is the only of you four in a relationship and that Sean isn't good enough for her."

Jack's heart warmed at the way she automatically referred to him as one of her own. And then stuttered contemplating if the Taylors would consider him good enough for their youngest daughter. He cleared his throat and shifted in his seat.

Cam rolled his eyes. "You know I'm never getting married, and guilt doesn't work, Mom. Moving on––my focus is on all the foundational items. Right now, there's a lot going on with the Coastal Commission and simple building issues. If we're going to make our May opening date, I need to stay on track."

"What he said." Campbell flashed a cheeky grin and pointed a finger at Cam. "My brother the romantic. But back to you guys, are you sure you're feeling okay after the accident? I'm surprised that you chose to travel so soon."

"We were lucky, sweetie." Her dad patted her shoulder. "Well, except for your mom's wrist. The insurance company is taking care of everything, and we'll get a new car in the next week or so. But we have important news and won't allow the accident to derail us any more than necessary."

Before he could elaborate, a scarlet-haired waitress in head-to-toe black stepped up. She scanned the table, her dark eyes gleaming with interest when they landed on Jack. "Hello everyone, my name is Gabriela and I'll be taking care of you tonight. Can I bring you something to drink?"

Even though she spoke to "everyone," she was checking him out. Great, just what he needed tonight. Jack studied the menu, careful not to catch her eye.

"We were waiting for my daughter to order the wine, she's a sommelier," Clyde said.

"Hi Gabriela, I'm Campbell Taylor, I think we met at an event last month." Campbell's lips curved up in a smile. "We would love to start with a bottle of the 2017 Law Beguiling Grenache blend."

Jack gazed up and the waitress was studying him and Campbell. Assessing. Her lips curved upward. "We did. Lovely to see you again. Are you all celebrating something special tonight?"

Mrs. T piped in, "We absolutely are——my husband and I have a surprise for our children."

The waitress stared at Jack for a long moment before responding. "Wonderful. I'll make sure to take extra-special care of you all. Tonight's specials are listed on a separate sheet in the regular menu. I can answer any questions for you when I return with the wine." She inclined her head and headed back into the restaurant.

Clyde chuckled and smacked the table. "Oh Jack, that one couldn't keep her eyes off you. Nothing has changed. Good thing Campbell is here to protect you from all the women who fall at your feet."

"Don't embarrass Jack. He can't help it if women get googly-eyed around him," Mrs. T said.

Campbell frowned. "She was just being friendly, Dad."

"I'd say that Jack won't find a shortage of dates in his new hometown." Cam smirked.

Jack held up his hands. "Stop it all of you." Inwardly, he winced. Time to redirect the conversation.

He leaned forward. "Okay, let's focus on your big news. What, are you two retiring, selling your house, and traveling the country in an RV or something?"

Christine held up a hand. "Well, something like that. We are retiring from the school. No more full-time teaching and your father's tired of being a principal. We are selling the house, but under no circumstances will we ever get an RV. You know the cat and dogs wouldn't stand for that lifestyle and frankly, neither would I." She gave a faux shudder.

Campbell whipped her head between her parents. "Retiring already? You're only 60."

Clyde nodded and continued, "We decided we wanted to live somewhere quieter than Redwood City. The urban sprawl over the last twenty years has changed everything. So, drumroll please, we bought a little fixer-upper cottage in Pacific Grove, so we'll be close to Cam and much closer to you two." Mr. Taylor's lean face split into a grin and his deep blue eyes twinkled.

Cam tensed and his fingers gripped his water glass tight enough his knuckles went white. So, the news shocked him too. And knowing Cam the way he did, his buddy probably assumed his parents wanted to move closer because of his permanent injury.

Cam's brow furrowed. "Are you guys ready to retire? I mean, financially?"

"We've been really smart with our money and do have pensions. Having Camille as our personal financial advisor helps. And the fact you kids went to college on scholarships allowed us to sock away a nice nest egg, even on our paltry salaries. Trust me, we're not going to be living in the lap of luxury. But we'll be somewhere peaceful and close to our children, which is what matters at the end of the day." Mrs. T's eyes sparkled.

"And I've got a few ideas of part-time projects to dabble in." Mr. Taylor winked.

Campbell clapped her hands together, then turned and hugged each of her parents in turn. "I think this is amazing. I love that you'll be living down on the Central Coast near Cam and Jack."

Her mom tilted her head. "And what about you, honey? You're based here too, right?"

"Well, at least for the next year. But if—" She paused and cleared her throat. "*When* I become a Master Som, there may be some opportunities too good to pass up. I mean, if I have a chance to be a Beverage Director at a Michelin Star restaurant in Paris or Milan..." Campbell's smile faltered.

Jack inhaled a steadying breath and reached for his water, wishing it was wine. Every time Campbell mentioned she might be leaving next year, his gut clenched.

Time to screw his head on straight. They had kissed one time. Once. Despite his undeniable attraction to her, there wouldn't be a repeat. One and done. They were friends, practically family. Period.

Campbell laid a hand on her dad's forearm. "Well, Camille

still lives in the Bay Area. What about her? Is she moving too?"

Her mom shook her head. "Your sister travels so much for her job and is happy where she is. We'll probably see her more now because she'll have to visit."

Their other daughter worked for one of the big accounting firms and so did this slick trust-fund guy, Sean, the boyfriend nobody liked. Jack hadn't been as close to Camille because she'd gone to college in Boston and hadn't always returned to California for holidays.

For a moment, an awkward silence lingered over the table. The tic in Cam's cheek revealed his irritation. He had a classic poker face but even he couldn't control that tell.

Time to smooth out the situation. "Well, I'm excited because I'm pretty sure that means I get to have Thanksgiving dinner with you every year again, right?" Over the last decade, he'd not been able to return as often for his favorite holiday.

Christine beamed. "Absolutely. Starting with this year because we're moving at the end of October."

"That's great, Mom. It will be wonderful to be closer to you both." Campbell smiled and picked up her menu. "We should probably figure out what we're going to have for dinner."

Jack perused the menu and his mouth watered. One more reason he was looking forward to living in wine country full-time--the amazing food. "Any recommendations, Campbell?"

Her beautiful eyes lit up. "Every single dish I've ever had is incredible. The grilled octopus is divine, and they're known for the Pasta al nero di sepia con granchio: squid in pasta with Dungeness crab. And if you're in the mood for steak, you can't go wrong with the filet mignon."

"Have you had this Ravioli mais dolce? I've never heard of

sweet corn ravioli before, and with mushrooms?" Mrs. T turned to her daughter with raised brows.

"It's delicious. This restaurant is already one of my favorites," Campbell said.

The waitress returned and presented the bottle with a flourish to Campbell. Once everyone's glasses were filled, they ordered. Cam was his customary stoic self.

Jack and Campbell kept the conversation lively, on all types of topics unrelated to living arrangements. Then, the busboy removed their plates and offered dessert menus. So far, so good.

"I'd love to see your new places. What if we grab some gelato and head over to one of your apartments for dessert and coffee?" Clyde said.

Campbell jolted. "Oh no, they've got the most incredible tiramisu here. And I hate to admit it, but I'm exhausted and I'd planned on hitting the books again tonight--"

"Oh honey, I'm sorry if we cut into your study time. We were so excited to tell you about our move." Clyde patted Campbell's shoulder.

"I'm a little tired too and we have to drive back to Monterey. We'll make plans to come see your apartments some other time. And I do love tiramisu," Christine said.

"Please don't apologize. I'm thrilled to see you all. It's just…"

Cam lifted one hand. "It's fine. We'll head out from here. I was thinking of coming down next week to see the progress of Maison du Soleil. When are the guys and Charlie coming up?"

Jack stiffened. No way in hell could Cam come down next week. "The entire county is at full capacity for people working the crush. It will be at least a few weeks."

"Don't you have a lot to do in Monterey?" Campbell asked.

Cam's brows drew together as he looked between them. "Well, I can still come earlier too, right? One of you has to have a couch I can crash on, don't you?"

Jack caught Campbell's gaze and silently communicated that he'd handle it. "Yeah, but it's not ideal right now. I don't want you to waste your time because we're definitely going to need you later."

"Huh." Cam's jaw clenched. "I don't need special treatment. I'm perfectly fine to sleep on the floor or couch."

A crease formed between Campbell's brows. "Cam, it isn't about you, okay?"

Luckily, the waitress reappeared for their dessert orders before Cam could respond. Jack sighed. Tonight was like navigating a minefield between offending his friend and trying not to lie to all the Taylors.

Mrs. T, accustomed to her son's moods, ignored Cam's glowering expression and asked Jack some real estate questions over dessert. Thank god. Anything to keep the evening on track.

Jack snagged the check and insisted on treating. After they said their goodbyes, Jack's pulse regulated––they'd pulled it off.

Once he and Campbell returned to the apartment, she crossed to the kitchen and pulled two wineglasses from the cabinet. "Well, that didn't have any awkward moments at all. No awkward moments at all."

"I think the only challenge was Cam. But he already was in one of his moods," Jack said.

"Yeah, he definitely was. And we both know why." She uncorked a bottle of red. "Want another glass of wine?"

"I thought you had to study?" Which would be safer for them both. His heart thudded against his ribcage.

"It's not happening tonight. I'm going to have a glass. I

can have it in the bedroom or share it with you out here." She glanced over her shoulder, her ice blue eyes wide.

He winced--there was *bedroom* and *sharing* again. "Sure, I'll have some. But I don't want to be the reason you don't hit the books."

"You aren't the reason. I'm processing about Cam." She poured the wine, set down his glass on the coffee table, and sipped her Syrah.

"Yeah, he assumes your parents are moving down because he needs help and that doesn't sit well with him." Jack rubbed one hand across the scruff on his jaw.

She settled onto the couch next to him, a hint of her floral scent teasing him. "Exactly. I know he's devastated but I'm so grateful he's alive and he's home. It's awful that he lost part of his leg, but his prosthetic is so good, it's only obvious to him."

Jack blew out a breath. "I don't think either of us can imagine. All he ever wanted was a military career. But working on the Monterey hotel is a challenge and being part of the Hotel Kings is a second chance."

She tilted her head toward him. "Yeah, the hotels are more than business for all of us."

"That's the truth." He massaged the taut muscles on the back of his neck. If the team thought he was only crashing on Campbell's couch, it would contradict his claims he was serious about finally settling down. And if everyone knew how much he wanted her? A full-blown disaster.

She rose from the couch and gazed at him. "And on that note, I'd better go to bed because I've got study group tomorrow. I hope you get a good night's sleep."

"Goodnight." Somehow, he figured a good night's sleep wasn't in the cards for him. Not on the lumpy mattress. Not with his imagination running wild fantasizing about what Campbell was doing in the next room. Again.

CHAPTER 8

Campbell's temples throbbed. She'd tossed and turned last night, memories of Jack's kisses haunting her. She was exhausted, confused, and not in the mood to deal with crap from Roger the snobby sommelier. Studying with a local group made sense and Sylvia was great. Roger--not so much.

Maybe it was the way he peered down his imperious nose or cleared his throat between every single sip of wine before making some obvious pronouncement, as if she and Sylvia hadn't reached the same conclusion. Or how when he'd learned she'd come from a middle-class suburban upbringing, he treated her like she was beneath him.

He'd made some snide comment about the requirement that Master Sommeliers had to have impeccable social skills, not the kind one gained in public school. Pompous little trust-fund baby. If Xavier hadn't insisted she work with him, she would have ended the arrangement after their first session. The guy personified the worst of the worst in the male-dominated industry.

There were only a handful of women Master Sommeliers

in the world and certain men wanted to keep it that way. Of the 144 Master Sommeliers in the U.S., only 28 were women. More women were entering the wine industry and climbing the ranks, but some men didn't want to acknowledge that most women's palates were superior, including her own. She loved her chosen vocation and most days the positives outweighed the negatives.

Some days she didn't have the energy to deal with the Rogers. Like today.

"Earth to Campbell. Did you hear a word I said about the 2017 varietals, or do you already know everything?" Roger's nasal voice penetrated her musings.

Annoyance flared through her. "Of course I don't know everything. I thought we were doing some blind tastings of the Burgundies and Beaujolais and then flash cards, right? Not discussing 2017 right now."

Sylvia nodded and smoothed back a strand of ebony hair into the classic chignon she favored. "That's correct. I suggest we do the flash cards first and then the tastings. Does that work for you both?" Thank goodness Sylvia was even-tempered and diplomatic.

Campbell took a cleansing breath and forced the corners of her mouth to turn up. Probably more of a grimace than a smile, but she tried. "Flash cards, it is." Patience and an ability to deal with difficult personalities came with the territory.

Sylvia pulled a container of cards from her briefcase and set them on the weathered oak table in the conference room of the Salis Farms Winery, a gorgeous property owned by her parents.

Because Sylvia didn't want to run the family winery, she was seeking her Master Sommelier so she could travel the world instead. Her knowledge of the viticulture aspects of winemaking were impressive. Plus, she was nice and didn't make it feel like she was in direct competition for a spot, like Roger.

For the next few hours, Campbell was able to focus on the world's wine regions and varietals. Her memory wasn't technically a photographic one––wouldn't that be amazing––but she could retain knowledge as if the information was time-stamped in her brain. Maybe today wouldn't be a complete failure, after all.

After a quick break, they set up the wines for the afternoon's blind-tasting. Halfway through, Campbell messed up. She couldn't place one varietal and even got the tasting notes incorrect. For some reason the White Burgundy didn't have the customary notes of peach and citrus and she'd called it wrong. She was off her game.

"Do you want to try again?" Sylvia's deep brown eyes were kind.

She wanted to throw in the towel for the day but she took a steadying breath––she could do this.

"She missed it, okay? She doesn't need a do-over."

Campbell's fingers curled into fists, her nails digging into her palms. "Seriously Roger, what is your problem?"

He rolled his eyes behind his pretentious horn-rims, which were probably clear glass, a prop to try to look more intelligent. "Fine, do you want to know what my problem is? I'll tell you. You've got no place here. You're an adequate sommelier. But we all know you're the token beach bimbo in the upcoming class of candidates and you'll never make it."

"Roger!" Sylvia's jaw dropped. "Enough."

Campbell's nostrils flared. "Token beach bimbo? What, because I was a collegiate soccer player? Because I have blonde hair? Just because you're only capable of doing one thing at a time––mind you, not particularly well––doesn't mean that others can't be stars in more than one sky. I am not only smarter than you, but I'm also socially intelligent, which is something you are not."

She surged to her feet and started packing up her bag. "Sylvia, I apologize. I will not work with this ass another minute."

Sylvia rose and pointed at Roger. "Xavier is going to hear about this. Pack up your things and go. You're not welcome here any longer. Campbell and I will find another third."

She blew out a breath and turned to Campbell. "Let me walk you out."

Campbell's legs trembled, not from fear or weakness, but with fury. Yes, she'd made mistakes today but that didn't mean she was inferior. Why did the Rogers of the world look down on her because she was an athletic blue-eyed blonde from California? Many people assumed her University of California, Berkeley scholarship was for soccer, when in fact it was for academics.

She didn't bother to correct them. If they wanted to underestimate her, that was their issue, not hers. But sometimes, it really ticked her off. Like now.

"Are you okay?" Sylvia patted her shoulder. "You know he's full of it, right? You've got one of the most gifted palates of anyone vying for Master Sommelier and he's jealous because he has to work so hard for something that comes naturally to you."

Campbell's shoulders softened from where they'd crept up by her ears. "Thanks. I apologize for not being one hundred percent today. And sometimes the egos in this industry get to me."

Sylvia's lips turned down. "Well, me, too. I mean people assume I have an in or something because of my family's winery. Like that will help me pass the exam. And that guy is next level. Maybe that's why Xavier suggested we work with him? To practice not allowing the jerks to shake our composure. You know some of those old timers will probably be unpleasant during the service exam."

The knots in Campbell's belly loosened. "You know what, that makes so much sense. Great point. And every industry has its challenges."

Sylvia nodded. "Isn't that the truth? And Roger's gotten more airtime than he's worth. Tell me how things are going with Maison du Soleil."

As they crossed toward the massive oak tree underneath where Campbell's Volvo was parked, she dug out her sunglasses. "Everything is moving along according to plan. Well, you know how renovation deadlines go. It's going to be incredible."

She opened her door, allowing the baking heat inside her car a chance to dissipate. It was in the high-90s today, the sun's rays unrelenting in a sapphire sky.

"I'd love to come up and see it sometime. Will you buy a house closer to West Paso?"

Campbell's shoulders tensed again. "I'm not even considering moving until after the hotel opens and until I've passed all three exam levels next year."

"Makes sense. What are you up to now? Want to go get a glass of wine?" Sylvia grinned and help up her hands. "To drink, not to dissect."

Campbell smiled, warmed by the easy camaraderie she'd developed in a short time with Sylvia. "I didn't sleep well last night, so I'm going to pass. But let's definitely do something next week?"

"Sure. I can always pop by next time I'm closer to town?"

Campbell froze. One more complication with her and Jack's living situation. "Oh, my place is a shoebox. I can come out here or we can meet up at one of the wine bars?"

Sylvia gave her a quick hug. "I want to get away from here

for a night, so a bar it is. I'll text you later. And erase this afternoon from your mind, okay?"

"Thanks, girl. You're the best."

CAMPBELL PARKED NEXT to Jack's Land Rover. He'd beaten her back to the apartment from Maison du Soleil. Or maybe he was out running or hiking or doing something that didn't require his car. All she wanted to do was blast the air-conditioning, pop some popcorn, and veg out on the couch in front of the TV. No thinking required. Bolstered by the thought of some alone time, she unlocked the front door and headed into her little sanctuary.

But her sanctuary was anything but a haven right now. The Murphy bed was down and out and so was Jack. He was sprawled on his belly, his face buried in a pillow. His sleekly muscled back was bare, and those gray sweatpants only emphasized the perfection that was his ass. But his appearance wasn't what caught her attention.

The only sound in the icebox of an apartment——had he turned it down to 40 degrees or something? ——was the sawing of logs. The roaring of lions.

Jack snored.

Jack snored really loud.

She giggled and clapped a hand over her mouth. Mr. Gorgeous Charming Smooth-Talking Tall Drink of Water snored like an ogre who would terrify children or the wolf who would blow down the three little pigs' houses. For some reason, she didn't remember him snoring when he'd stayed with her family. Granted, Cam's basement bedroom could have masked this cacophony.

She tip-toed to the kitchen island and gingerly placed her messenger bag on the quartz countertop. Time to implement her immediate plot for future revenge. They'd played pranks on each other back when she was a teenager and old habits die hard.

First, she opened the video button on her smartphone and raised the volume up to maximum decibels. Then, she slid off her sandals and tip-toed toward the couch. She tapped the red record button and crouched so the camera was level with Jack's face and let it roll. He didn't budge. After a minute or so, she clicked her phone off. She had plenty of footage to use as a negotiating tool should Jack deserve a little taunting.

Show time. "Jack, you up?"

He grunted and shifted, but the long black lashes on his cheek didn't even flutter.

"Jack," she yelled.

He sprang up to a seated position, his head swinging from side to side. "What? What's happening?"

She hooted and waved her phone. "Wake up, Sleeping Beauty. You are the loudest snorer in the history of snorers, and I've got it on film."

He flipped her off and then scrubbed his hands through his short dark hair. "I was taking a nap."

She rolled her eyes. "I'm aware. How did I not know you sounded like a herd of charging buffaloes? Is that why you've lived alone since college and the army?"

"Turn off the video camera, Taylor." He dropped his head in his hands and leaned his elbows onto his powerful thighs.

Mirth filled her, erasing the tension from the last twenty-four hours. "It's off. It's off. And oh, is it pure gold. If you think for one minute that I've forgotten what you and Cam did the second time you came to stay with us––that would be Christmas––you are sorely mistaken." She sauntered to the kitchen counter and set her phone down.

He lifted his head his crystal-green eyes wide. "Are you

kidding? That was almost twenty years ago. And it was a harmless prank. We were teenagers."

She wagged a finger at him. "You two put food coloring in my shampoo and when I took the towel off my head my hair was neon green. It took a week to get it completely out and I had to keep a hat on for all the Christmas photos. Even the ones at the breakfast table. I told you I'd get you back." She grinned evilly.

He rose from the couch, and her laughter dried up, along with her throat. His bare torso was sheer perfection. Greek god-worthy––like those Olympic beach volleyball players–– sculpted symmetrical muscles covered with silky smooth skin.

He held up both hands. "Look, I know you got us back. The next year, right? When you put salt in the sugar bowl, and we used it on our cereal?"

She shook her head. "No, I did not. That was Camille's revenge for putting the cherry red coloring in her shampoo."

His full lips parted. "Oh. Well. Be reasonable––you can't share that video without admitting you were lurking next to the bed while I was sleeping."

Valid point. "You're such a lawyer." She frowned.

"Well, yeah. And the video could negatively impact the hotel," Jack cajoled, his lips quirking up at the corners.

"But I could send it to one of your dates, couldn't I? A little warning of what she might be getting into." And why did her chest tighten at the idea of him dating someone?

Jack huffed. "Look, my entire life for the next several months is opening up the hotel. No time to date." He strode purposefully toward her, one square-palmed hand extended. "Give me the phone."

She giggled and backed away. "No way."

He stalked her until she was backed up against the cool surface of the stainless-steel refrigerator. She held the phone behind her back, her shoulders shaking with laughter.

He stopped mere inches from her and caged her in, both hands braced on the refrigerator above her head. "Give me the phone."

The laughter died when she gazed up at him. "I'll give you the phone if you kiss me."

"Campbell, we can't do this." His pupils flared, the onyx crowding out the pale green. Her eyes dropped to his mouth and the desire to nip his full lower lip surged through her.

"Why not? We're attracted to each other. We're both single. We're both capable of being professional at work while we enjoy ourselves at home. If you don't want me, just say so." Her skin was tingling and heat flashed through her.

Her brain emptied and only need remained. Need for his mouth on hers. Need for him.

He closed his eyes and his jaw tightened. "You make it sound so simple."

She pressed one hand against his hard chest and his heart hammered against her palm, the staccato rhythm matching hers. "It can be."

He dropped his forehead against hers. "It's a really bad idea." But he didn't budge.

She slid her hands up around his neck and inhaled his clean masculine scent. "Probably. But right now, I don't care. It's our secret. It seems simple to me."

"There's nothing simple about it and you know it." His voice was raspy, his smooth skin hot beneath her fingertips.

"Please." Nothing else mattered but Jack. Not with him so close. Not in this moment, right here and right now.

He growled low in his throat and clasped her face in his strong hands. Slowly, oh so slowly, he lowered his head and slanted his mouth against hers.

Her insides liquefied and she drove her fingers into his

crisp, cropped hair. Their tongues tangled and danced, his warm breath mingling with hers. Sparks danced up her spine and she arched against him. His hands were everywhere, stroking down her back and clasping her waist, holding her in place.

Finally.

CHAPTER 9

*H*is self-control snapped. He slid one hand up and freed her fragrant hair from its ponytail. The soft strands spilled in sweet-smelling waves, and he wrapped his hand around the silky length and tugged. Screw the consequences.

She returned his kiss as fiercely as he gave and crushed her breasts against him. Her sweet, honeyed taste, the heat simmering off her satiny skin, and her uninhibited response drove him mad. Unable to stop now, he pulled her shirt off and tossed it over his shoulder. He drew in a harsh breath at the vision of her creamy breasts. Her pink nipples tightened into taut peaks.

"Touch me. Please." Her eyes were heavy-lidded. Her lips were swollen from their kisses.

His mind emptied. He cupped her breasts and brushed his thumbs back and forth and she moaned deep in her throat.

He had to taste her. He lowered his head and flicked her nipple with his tongue, then tugged on it with his teeth. He groaned––he'd never sampled anything so delicious.

Her hips bucked, slamming into him. Without lifting his

mouth, he dragged her legs up and she wrapped them around his waist, her center burning into him.

"More." Her fingernails dug into his shoulders and her head dropped back, exposing her slender ivory neck.

He trailed kisses up to the hollow in her throat, where her pulse thrummed beneath his lips.

"Hold on tight." He tightened his grip, pivoted away from the cold steel of the refrigerator, and tumbled them onto the Murphy bed.

"Ouch. Wow, you weren't kidding about this bed." A laugh escaped her.

He rolled them over, so she was on top. "Told you so. But I don't usually dive onto it."

He couldn't take his eyes off her——tousled platinum hair, tight rosy nipples, and slender curves.

"Hmm… I like this view." She stroked her hands across his chest, leaned down, and brushed her lips across his skin, each touch scorching him.

She kissed and licked down his chest to his abs. When she reached the waistband of his pants, she peeked up at him, her blue eyes gleaming. She wrapped her fingers around his hard length.

Any remaining thoughts, protests, and blood flew from his brain and pooled below his waist. He moaned when she pushed his sweats down and grasped him in both hands.

His breath caught and her name came out on a hiss. "Campbell."

"Shh." Her pink lips curved upward without breaking their locked gaze, then she lowered her head and licked him from base to tip. He bowed up and dug his hands into the sheets.

Unable to look away, his muscles tensed and jumped while she took her sweet time tasting and teasing him. His pulse pounded in his temples and sweat slicked his skin.

She lifted her head and met his gaze. Without a word, she wrapped her lips around him and took him deep, until he reached the back of her throat.

"Fuck." He gritted out and his hands reached for her hair--not controlling the pace but holding on while she licked and sucked and blew his mind. Pure pleasure flooded through him but when his lower back started to tingle, he gently pulled her hair. "Campbell, let me kiss you."

She hesitated then kissed her way back to his lips, sliding her bare breasts against him, hot and achingly soft. He wrapped his arms around her and rolled them so she was beneath him, bracing his forearms on either side of her.

She gazed up and her teeth dug into her full lower lip. "How did that feel?"

"You're incredible. That felt incredible." He captured her mouth, sinking into her. "My turn."

She smiled and stretched her arms overhead, like a kitten waking up from an afternoon nap. She was so damn sexy and confident, and he couldn't wait a second longer to taste her.

He shifted to lay beside her and trailed his fingers along her hot skin and cupped her through the thin material of her pants. "Clothes off now," she murmured, her head falling to the side, her eyes closed.

He dragged them down--thank god for elastic waists-- and his heart stuttered when he saw the tiny scarlet slip of lace she'd been wearing beneath her loose linen trousers.

"Oh my god, you're so ready for me." He groaned and thrust one finger inside her, then a second, stroking in a rhythm that made her purr. When he pressed his thumb against her, she rocked into his hand.

His mouth traveled across her soft skin, nuzzling the tender underside of her breasts before continuing down the trembling flat planes of her belly. She undulated beneath his touch, more responsive than he could have dreamed. He was so hard it hurt but giving her pleasure was his first priority.

He pressed open mouthed kisses along her hipbones, lightly scraping his teeth over her sensitive flesh.

"Your mouth is so incredible, Jack. Oh my god." Her voice was throaty.

"I cannot wait to taste you," he murmured against her skin before licking her with one, long firm stroke.

Her spine bowed. He grasped her hips and held her in place. He circled his tongue over her sensitive bud and thrust one finger inside her, then another. Her sweet scent surrounded him and she tasted like heaven. Tremors pulsated through her.

She froze, dug her fingers into his hair. "Jack. Don't stop. Oh my god, yes."

Once she'd finished chanting his name, he took his time kissing up her body to capture her mouth. Her kiss was hot, intense.

She drew back and murmured against his lips, "Please tell me you have protection."

He lifted his head and gazed into her heavy-lidded eyes. "Give me a second." He levered off the bed and stalked to grab his wallet. Offered thanks when he found the packet.

He returned to the bed and paused for a moment; his breath lodged in his throat. She was glorious, a silvery goddess framed on rumpled sheets. He ripped open the foil and rolled on the condom without breaking her gaze.

"Hurry. I want you." She beckoned with one slender hand.

Like there was any way in hell he could stop now. He lowered his weight, settling between her long legs. "I want you too, sweetness."

"Now. Please." She dug her nails into his shoulders.

His entered her slowly, inch by inch, her heat gripping him like a glove. He slid home and she wrapped her legs around his waist. "Give me a moment--you're huge." She whispered against his throat.

"Am I hurting you?" He paused and pushed up to his forearms.

"No, stay right where you are and kiss me." She dug her heels into his lower back, holding him immobile.

He stroked her cheek, then captured her mouth. Sweat beaded on his brow, but her sweet breath and deep kisses burned through him.

"Now. Slowly please," she whispered, her voice throaty.

He began to move and together they found a slow, dreamy rhythm--each stroke exquisite torture. She felt incredible. She felt like home.

His eyes almost rolled back in his head--the pleasure was so powerful. He deepened his pace and she matched him stroke for stroke, urging him on.

"I'm going to come." Wave after wave pulsed through her and she came apart, triggering his own release.

"I'm with you." He followed her over the edge. "Campbell."

For a few moments, the world stilled. He lifted his head and brushed her hair from her flushed face. He pressed a kiss against her lips, awe filling him.

She sighed against his mouth. "Wow."

His lips curved up. "Wow is right. Give me a minute to take care of this. Don't go anywhere." He stood and disposed of the condom.

He joined her on the bed and gathered her close. "You know it's still sunny outside, right?"

She giggled and hugged him. "It's Sunday afternoon and here we are in the Murphy bed. What should we do now?"

A quick stab of possessiveness shot through him, and he shoved it aside. No time to start thinking now. Not yet anyway. For now, he'd keep it light. "I don't know about you but I'm starving."

A flicker of vulnerability shadowed her eyes. "Me too. Let's order in and watch movies for the rest of the day. Tomorrow is soon enough to return to reality."

His lips quirked. "Should I put my bed back in the wall? Move to the couch for movie and pizza?"

She laughed again. "I am going to see that wall in a whole new light now. Yeah, let's order a giant pizza and some salad. I'll break out a good bottle--oh who am I kidding, all my bottles are great bottles--and we can see what's streaming. What are you in the mood for?"

To take you into the shower and fuck you against the wall. But right now, he wanted her to set the pace. If she wanted to slip back into friendship mode and watch movies on the couch, he'd do it.

"Jack?"

He shook his head. "I'm easy, but nothing dark or dramatic. Not after this last week."

She sat up and her cheeks flushed a gorgeous shade of pink. "Um, yeah. I'm going to put on some clothes. So should you."

"Campbell." He caught her hand before she bolted to her bedroom. "Are we okay?" He managed to keep his eyes above her lovely throat. Barely.

She caught her lower lip in her white teeth and nodded. "We are. But I'm not comfortable enough to hang out naked with you quite yet."

A little late after the mind-blowing sex, but no need to point that out. Nor was it the time to consider they hadn't even lasted one week before their attraction exploded.

He tugged her closer until they were again mere inches apart. "I may persuade you to slip out of those clothes later tonight. If that is okay with you."

She pressed her lips against his in a feather-light kiss. "You are awfully persuasive. We'll see how it goes. And I'm with you on the no-more-drama movie. Clothes first."

She rose and sauntered across the apartment, her hips swaying. Her confidence and beauty knocked into him like a tsunami. Campbell was one of a kind. Their history of friendship and family was solid, but this explosive passion between them was new and could change everything. Because she stoked something inside him he'd never felt before.

Because Campbell Taylor was dangerous. Dangerous to his equilibrium. Dangerous to his heart.

CHAPTER 10

By the time she closed the bedroom door, Campbell was certain the flush on her cheeks covered every inch of her body. She'd casually ambled across the room like it was no big deal, but her galloping pulse and shaky legs didn't disguise reality.

The reality was they'd just shared the most incredible sex of her life. The reality of Jack blew her schoolgirl fantasy of him out of the water.

How could she have known how perfectly they would fit together? How the slip and slide of their bare skin would generate the most beautiful friction. How the clean scent of his skin would stoke her desire even as the taste of him drove her wild?

And unlike other first times with a lover, their connection was deeper, more complete because of their history. Because they trusted each other. And somehow, after they'd come apart in each other's arms, they seemed to slip right back into that comfortable friendship they'd had forever. How was that possible? Because they cared about each other. Everything was going to be just fine.

She hurried to her dresser and whipped out a pair of her favorite shorts and a baggy high school soccer jersey. Her hair was a tangled mess, so she ran a comb through it and wound it into a messy bun on top of her head. When she checked in the mirror, despite the outfit and hair, her eyes gleamed, her cheeks were rosy, and her lips looked well-kissed.

When she returned to the living room, Jack lounged against a virtual nest of pillows and blankets on the Murphy bed, his leaf green eyes gleaming, his full lips in a half-smile. "Fully loaded large pizza and Caesar salad should be here in half an hour. Why doesn't Madam Sommelier come tell me which wine she will choose to complement the gourmet meal?"

Damn, he looked sexy reclining in those sweatpants. He really needed to put on a shirt or she might not be trusted to wait until after dinner to pounce on him again.

She pursed her lips and spoke in her best snooty faux accent. "Ah oui oui monsieur, this evening, I have zee perfect bottle pour vous. No need to worry about the title and year, you are in perfect hands with me." She waggled her eyebrows.

He chuckled. "Oh, your hands are perfect all right. But come here first so we can choose the movie. I've got it narrowed down." He patted the bed next to him.

A shiver of awareness sparked through her. She crossed the space between them, a flutter dancing in her belly. It was just Jack. But it was *Jack*. Her fantasy guy in her place, with eyes only for her. Her throat grew parched, but she strove to appear casual. To live in the moment.

She hesitated by the edge of the mattress. He grasped her hand and tugged her down onto the soft pile of sheets and blankets next to him. Heat flared in her belly and she melted against him, running her fingertips along his firm defined pecs and taut abs.

She pressed a kiss on his velvety skin. "Someone missed me."

He growled and one hand slipped down to cup her ass. "Watching you strut into your bedroom has given me some very interesting ideas."

Goosebumps leapt up on her skin and she shifted so they were eye to eye. "Oh really?"

"Mmm-hmm." He lowered his mouth to hers, then jolted back when a loud noise burst between them.

"What is that?" She looked around.

"The remote control." Jack grabbed the offending piece of plastic and clicked off the blaring television.

Talk about a way to douse the passion—the evening news squawking from the wide-screen TV. Campbell slid off the bed and padded into the kitchen. She'd open the wine to keep her hands occupied before the food arrived.

He rose and joined her at the counter, looking tousled and a little grumpy. "What can I do to help?"

So, she wasn't the only one disappointed at the interruption. "Turn on the TV again, on mute please, and pick the movie?"

He muttered under his breath but complied.

She pivoted to the wine refrigerator and crouched down to contemplate her choices. A Chianti Classico always suited pizza and salad. She had a few bottles from Italy that a wine salesman had sent her to potentially carry at Maison du Soleil. If she decanted it now, it would open up beautifully by the time the food arrived.

She filled the engraved decanter her parents had given her when she'd passed her first level sommelier exam a few years ago. Task complete and a hint of composure regained, she glanced at Jack, who looked like some kind of Greek God reclining on the pillows. His smooth light brown skin, his carved from marble physique, and his chiseled jawline added up to one gorgeous man.

Another flush of arousal coursed through her, simply from looking at him. And for tonight, he was all hers. She returned to the bed. "Someone looks like the cat who swallowed the cream."

She slid onto the sheets and in one swift move, he cradled her in the circle of his powerful arms. "Oh, I'd say I'm pretty pleased with life right now. And I found the perfect movie."

She slid her arms around his neck and the heat from his bare skin burned through the thin material of her ancient jersey. He cupped her face in his hands and slowly lowered his mouth to hers, their tongues winding against each other with a languid rhythm, like they had all the time in the world to explore each other's taste. He growled her name.

She stroked one hand down along his broad shoulder, along his hard chest and ridged abdominals. He sucked in a sharp inhale and caught her hand before she reached the waistband of his sweats. "The food will be here any minute."

She pouted. "You're choosing pizza over me?"

His stomach rumbled. "Never. But for one, when I get you naked again, nothing's going to interrupt us. And two, as you can hear, I'm ravenous. And three, you're going to be so excited when you find out what movie I found for us, you'll forgive me."

"Huh." He did have a point. But still.

A loud knocking solved their dilemma.

"I've got it." Jack rolled off the bed and strode to the door. He tipped the delivery girl, crossed to the kitchen island, and set down a ridiculously large pizza box and the salad.

"Eat at the counter or watch the movie?" Campbell joined him and poured the wine.

"Let's eat while we watch the movie." Jack stuffed half a

slice in his mouth and transferred the woodfired pizza onto a large platter and divvied up the salad into two bowls in record time.

Once they got situated against the cushions, Jack wielded the remote like it was a magic wand. "You ready?"

She nibbled on her pizza and moaned. "Oh my god, this pizza is so good."

His pupils dilated. "You keep making sounds like that and we'll never make it through the whole thing."

She fluttered her eyelashes. "I mean, intermissions are a good thing, right? So, what did you pick?"

He clicked the remote and the opening scene of *The Princess Bride* appeared on the screen.

Her heart melted and she clapped her hands together. "You remembered." It was her favorite movie.

"Well, you did force us to watch it every Thanksgiving weekend." He grinned.

"And you loved it every time." Even though her brother teased her about it, Jack had memorized all the lines right along with her.

"I did. Who doesn't love this movie? I know it's been a tough week, and this movie always made you smile." He grinned.

Her belly took a long slow flop. "Jack Cassidy. I never imagined you'd be so sentimental." She'd been crushing on him so hard in those early days and had no idea if he'd ever suspected.

A crease formed between his dark brows. "What do you mean you never imagined?" He took another bite of pizza and gestured with one hand for her to continue.

She covered her mouth with her hand. *Oh crap.* "Oh nothing. In general. You know. Some people are sentimental. Others aren't so sentimental. That's all." She waved a hand, all nonchalant and such.

His eyes narrowed. "No, that's not what you meant. You're a terrible liar. Tell me."

Her fingers trembled as she sipped her wine. And decided what the hell. "Fine. I'll tell you."

She cleared her throat. "So maybe I had a little crush on you in high school. And maybe I imagined what you would be like if we dated."

His full lips parted, and a look of genuine surprise crossed his face. "You're kidding me."

She shook her head. "Nope. That first weekend you came home with Cam, I was tongue-tied. I'd never cared about boys and then you showed up. You were my first crush."

"Aww, Campbell. I thought all you cared about back then was soccer and books. I had no idea." His lips curved up.

She laughed, more relaxed now. "Of course you didn't. Nobody knew but me and my locked diaries."

"Diaries? You have a diary?" His eyes gleamed with mischief, and he looked around the room.

"Had. *Had* diaries." She held up a hand. "I don't have time for those anymore. Not to inflate your ego any more than it already is, but virginal 15-year-old Campbell had no concept of what you'd be like in bed. You definitely exceeded any fantasies."

He jumped up, grabbed the food, and tossed it on the counter. "I call intermission. Now."

A flare of heat surged through her, pooling low in her belly. "You're too funny. I thought you were starving."

"I've had enough pizza to fuel me for a bit. What I'm hungry for now is you." His voice was husky.

He picked up a condom, dove onto the bed, and rolled her on top of him again. He managed to tug her shirt over her head and skimmed his broad powerful hands up her spine, yanking her down until their bare skin melded together. He growled and nibbled up her neck, his mouth hot, his tongue teasing.

Goosebumps prickled along her skin everywhere his mouth traveled.

They were both impatient. Burning. Passionate.

When he reached between them and cupped her, she rocked against his hand. Seeking sensation. Craving more.

"Sweetness, you're so ready for me right now. Condom." He teased and caressed her, each touch driving her wild.

She reached for the foil packet, and together they sheathed him in record time.

Jack clasped her hips and positioned her above him. When she slid home in one long satisfying stroke, they both cried out. She leaned down and pressed her mouth to his, savored the fullness of him inside her, the taste of his hot kisses, and the sweat slicking their bodies.

Round two was as incredible as round one. And pizza always tasted good cold.

CHAPTER 11

At the butt-crack of dawn, Campbell slinked out of her bedroom where Jack still slept. Not that they'd done much actual sleeping last night. Despite her casual claims about an easy reversion to friendship, nerves fluttered in her belly–– nothing was the same.

Last night, she'd slept better in Jack's arms than she'd ever slept before. In college, one of her girlfriends swore the ultimate soulmate test was the ability to sleep deeply while spooning. She'd scoffed at Jennifer's theory because…*really?*

Anyway. When he'd spooned her, his long legs, with their sprinkling of crisp hair, formed a warm protective curve behind hers. His muscular arm fit just so around her waist, his square palm pressed to her belly. And his broad shoulder formed the perfect cushion for her neck and head. They'd fit together like they'd been designed that way.

Effortless. Connected. Natural.

Or scary as hell.

Time to gather her composure prior to her meeting with her mentor. She parked in front of Spearhead, her favorite coffee place, and dropped her forehead onto the steering wheel. Every muscle in her body ached, but the pain was worth the pleasure they'd shared. Her lips curved up--Jack's sexy scruff had scraped the skin around her mouth, but each kiss was worth looking like she'd had a chemical peel. A third shot of espresso would be necessary to sharpen her foggy brain and ignore her well-used muscles.

Accustomed to excelling despite working long hours, Campbell would treat today's meeting like any other. Although after the scene with Roger yesterday, it wouldn't be a simple check in. She huffed out a breath and headed inside.

After ordering her drink and a pain au chocolat, she slid into one of the corner wood booths at the mostly empty cafe. It was only 6:30, before the daily rush. She opened her laptop, to review notes and ensure she was on track for the exam, take two. She nibbled on the pastry and closed her eyes in ecstasy--nothing beat the combination of warm chocolate and flaky croissant.

Her phone buzzed. Jack. Well, maybe some things were tastier than breakfast pastries.

Was I snoring?

Her lips curved upward. *Did you check online for the video?* Too easy to tease him.

YOU WOULDN'T DARE!!!!

She snickered and glanced around the quiet coffeehouse. Nobody there to witness her cackling like a hyena. Text flirting with Jack Cassidy was fun.

No need to yell. Of course I didn't. And no, you weren't snoring. I have an early meeting and you were sleeping like a baby. Although she'd been tempted to wake him and not only to share morning coffee.

Three bubbles appeared and disappeared on her screen.

Appeared. Disappeared.

Blank screen.

Finally, the third set of bubbles—*I see how you are. Have a great day. I'll pick up dinner tonight.*

Campbell's shoulders softened and her heart squeezed. She texted a thumbs up and placed her phone on the repurposed wood table. Could she handle all work by day and all Jack by night?

SEVERAL HOURS LATER, Xavier Nolan slid his wire-framed spectacles off and pinched the bridge of his hawklike nose.

Crap. Whenever her beloved mentor removed his glasses, it meant trouble. Campbell had only experienced his disappointment directed toward her once and she'd sworn not to face it again. She straightened in her seat, clasped her hands together tightly, and struggled to still her tapping foot.

He cleared his throat and replaced his glasses. "That's enough for today. Maybe we should have discussed the situation with Roger first because you don't seem to be yourself. But before we do, tell me if there's something else going on with you? Problems at your job? Are your parents okay after their accident?"

Double crap. Campbell winced. "No, everything with Hotel Kings is going well." The less she said, the better. So far, opening her mouth hadn't served her too well. She'd screwed up basic terroir questions and mixed up simple information despite knowing it inside and out.

"Well, then are you worried about your parents?"

Answering with a "no but I stayed up all night having wild passionate sex and I'm exhausted" wasn't an option. "My parents are fine, although my mom sprained her wrist. They came down to see me over the weekend, actually." She forced her lips to curve upward.

"I'm glad to hear it." He leaned forward, his artistic hands gripping the table between them. "You know I'm your biggest champion and you've got more potential as a Master Sommelier than anyone since Laura Williamson in the 90's. We've got to figure out how to keep you on track, because today's performance would result in you failing the exam again."

She bit the inside of her cheek. "Oh my goodness, Xavier. I apologize. Of course, I want this more than anything in the world. It's what I've worked toward for more than a decade. I will do better. I'm not making excuses, but this past week has been really tough."

"Part of this probably has to do with Roger, I'm sure. I spoke with him and Sylvia, so we don't have to discuss it, unless you want to. It can be helpful to work with difficult personalities, but he crossed the line and I'm going to reassign him. But know the examiners will be putting you and Sylvia under more scrutiny simply because you're women. They won't ask for explanations."

She swallowed, and much to her humiliation, blinked back moisture gathering in her eyes. Nobody had ever questioned her devotion to her craft. Digging her fingernails into her palms, she took a fortifying inhale.

"You're right, Xavier. I won't give you occasion to question my dedication again. I can't thank you enough for handling the situation with Roger." She stared into his sharp dark eyes.

He leaned back. "You're welcome. I know how much you've sacrificed and your usual work ethic. I believe in you, but you can't afford to have a bad day on the wrong day. Understand?"

She nodded. "I do. It won't happen again." Mistakes weren't an option. You either had what it took to move up to the elite or you didn't. And the handful of women who had made it certainly didn't make careless errors.

"Fine. Well, that's enough for today. Go do whatever you need to do to regain your focus. I recommend taking the evening off and getting a good night's sleep. Start fresh tomorrow."

She nodded again. "Of course. Maybe something as simple as eight hours sleep will make all the difference."

He stacked his notebooks and slid them into his battered army green briefcase. "You do that. And next week, show me the Campbell Taylor I've come to expect."

He strode from the library's reserved conference room. When the door clicked shut behind him, she exhaled a shaky breath and pressed her hands against her churning belly. Never in her wildest dreams had she thought she'd screw up like this. At least today hadn't been exam day.

Xavier's words seared into her soul. She rose and packed up her belongings––time to straighten out the situation. Temporary pleasure was not worth squandering her special gift or losing sight of her ambitions. Between her studies and her responsibilities with the hotels, there wasn't time for anything else.

For years, she'd worked her ass off pursuing her passion. She'd thrived under pressure and scrutiny, proven person after person wrong. Given up parties and trips with her girl-friends, like she had when she played soccer competitively. Purposefully kept her relationships casual, dedicating her energy for all things Master Sommelier.

Reciting the facts under her breath, she hurried to her car and slid behind the wheel.

Right now, her life was exactly where she wanted it––everything was on track. Since she'd discovered her passion for wine at that first diplomat dinner in Paris, she'd known. She would ace the exam on the second try and be set up to take the remaining two next year. She loved the challenges and rewards of her incredible job with the Hotel Kings.

An affair with Jack didn't fit into her plans.

If someone had told her when she was sixteen that she would have the best sex of her life with Jack Cassidy and then tell him it couldn't happen again, she would have laughed until she cried.

Her heart clenched in her chest. Not so funny now.

But nothing would stand in the way of her dreams. An affair with Jack was too risky.

They both had their priorities and committing to a significant other didn't top either of their lists. If she ended it now, they could slide back into their friendship and their perfect night would fade into the rear-view. A yummy memory, but distant, nonetheless.

After one night with Jack, she knew the more time she spent with him, the more she would fall for him. Her heart would shatter when it ended.

And it would definitely end. Jack was a great guy but wasn't known for long meaningful romantic relationships. Neither was she. Jack would understand.

Wouldn't he?

CHAPTER 12

Jack parked by the quaint center square of downtown Paso Robles--his new hometown--and hopped out of his car. A crisp breeze ruffled through the trees and prevented the heat from being oppressive. Barely. Despite operating on about two hours of sleep, energy pumped through his veins.

Even handling the five-hundred minor inconveniences of the day hadn't bothered him.

Window delivery delayed--no problem.

Shirt plastered to his back from the unrelenting sun on-site--all good.

Another permit in question with the county commission--just part of the job.

He sauntered to the craft eatery TASTE! to pick up the sliders and beet salads he'd ordered for dinner. Campbell had seemed confident they could navigate working and playing together. After last night, he was on board.

Like him, career was her number one priority. Like him, she wasn't looking for a serious relationship. With his pattern of moving every few years, he hadn't wanted to complicate his personal life. But they were consenting adults and his concerns about Cam and the guys no longer seemed like such a big deal.

She wasn't a hook-up or casual companion. They shared a foundation of true friendship and caring. Last night had been illuminating and their chemistry had blown his mind. Unlike the transitory nature of most of his relationships since law school, being with Campbell was like coming home. Tonight, they'd share an excellent meal and hang out. Keep it simple.

JACK PULLED up next to their condo, his fingers drumming on the steering wheel to the Rolling Stones belting out "Wild Horses". Dinner smelled mouthwatering and his stomach growled. Excitement flickered through him——he couldn't wait to see her, but he'd act cool and follow her lead.

He strode through the unlocked front door and crossed to the kitchen island. "Hey, I got us those sliders you were raving about."

Campbell sat at her small desk and angled her head slightly, "Oh yeah, thanks for doing that." Her voice was cool.

"Only fair and I'm starving." He began pulling out the take-out boxes, ignoring the pit forming in his gut.

She blew out a noisy exhale and stood, her back ramrod straight. "Jack, we need to talk."

So much for nothing changing. He gritted his teeth. "Sure. Can we talk over dinner?"

"It's important." She pivoted away from the desk and clasped her hands together.

He'd told himself he'd allow her to set the tone, but a frisson of annoyance flashed through him. "That's fine but like I said, I need to eat something now. So why don't you talk, and I'll start on my sliders, okay?"

Her nostrils flared and she nodded. "Fine." She marched to the other side of the kitchen, keeping the island of quartz between them.

He opened his takeout box--because he was damn hungry--picked up one of the sliders and gestured with it.

She pressed a hand to her throat. "Look, you were right about us getting involved being too complicated. I screwed up at my meeting with my mentor and it was a wake up call. I can't have any distractions outside of the hotel and studying. Not if I'm going to make Master Sommelier. We can't have a repeat of last night. I'm sorry."

He chewed on the beef slider with chevre, apricot jam and bacon, the marriage of flavors exploding on his tongue despite the brick in his belly. He swallowed. "Okay."

"Okay?" Her voice rose an octave.

Fuck it. "Okay. You're not the only one with priorities. You're not the only one who needs to avoid distractions. I'm responsible for ensuring Maison du Soleil opens without issue and on time. So, no repeat of last night."

Her artic blue eyes narrowed. "You're agreeing, just like that?"

His fingers tightened on the burger, and he tamped down the irritation. "Isn't my agreement what you wanted? Do you want to argue about it?" He ignored the twinge in the region of his chest.

She sighed and looked down at her hands. "You sound like such a lawyer. I don't want to argue, I thought--"

"Thought what, Campbell? I'm going along with what you want. And I am a lawyer by the way, so sorry if that's an issue with you now." No way in hell would he admit how damn happy he'd been all day and how much he'd looked forward to seeing her tonight.

"Look, I'm sorry. I couldn't focus because I was too busy thinking about..." A rosy flush stained her cheeks.

The same way her entire body bloomed pink when she was on the verge of coming apart. A memory he wouldn't be able to erase any time soon. His jeans suddenly felt uncomfortably tight. Great, like an erection would make this conversation less awkward.

"Campbell." Time to get a grip.

She met his gaze, her eyes unreadable. "You were right, okay? I don't think I can handle something casual, at least not with you."

"At least not with me?" He raised a brow.

She waved one hand. "Oh Jack, we have too much history, okay? That's why you avoided the apartment last week. You were right. And the most important thing to me right now is achieving what I've worked toward my entire career. I thought I could balance it all and obviously, I cannot. So, we need to have a plan."

With relentless self-control, he picked up a mushroom and cheddar slider and took a bite. His tone was smooth—classic Jack Cassidy. "Let's stay with our original plan. Some wineries' harvests end before others, so some space will free up in the next few weeks. Until then, let's minimize time here in the condo." No need to make this more difficult for her. For either of them.

She stared at him for a minute, a crease between her brows. "Just like that?"

"You sound disappointed." *I wish I could kiss that frown off your beautiful face.*

She squared her shoulders and shook her head. "I don't know what I expected. But fine. Dinner. Work. Friends."

"Yeah. Eat your sliders before they get cold. And you were right about the food—it's great." He took another bite and chewed casually, like his stomach wasn't churning. He'd file away that reaction to consider later.

Damn it, he would maintain his happy-go-lucky exterior

around her. Even though last night, it had felt incredible to feel free. To be with her fully. To experience the connection that flamed hot between them.

She circled around the counter and sat down next to him. "I'm sorry."

"Don't worry about it. Will it mess up your studying if I turn on Monday Night Football? I can watch it on mute."

She smacked his shoulder. "Don't be ridiculous. You don't have to watch it on mute. I'll watch some with you––I want to see the 49ers kick some ass. I'll study in my room afterwards. I've got silencing earphones, remember?"

"Well in that case, let me get the remote." He crossed to the coffee table and flipped on the TV. Watching football was safe. Nothing sexy about it.

"Great. And these sliders are incredible. The food in this town is the best."

He turned his stool to face the TV, no way was he sitting next to her on the couch. Nor would he pull down the Murphy Bed until she was safely tucked away in her room.

For now, he'd ensure they stayed in the friend zone.

How hard could it be?

CHAPTER 13

"*S*ee you tomorrow, Austin. And yes, we'll fit in some wine tasting. Never fear." She ended the call and parked next to Jack's Range Rover at Maison du Soleil.

Austin Michaels made her smile. The black sheep of the Michaels brothers, he was the only one of the Hotel Kings who hadn't attended San Diego State University on a ROTC scholarship. Boot camp and rock n' roll Austin would have clashed. Instead of attending college, Austin had pursued his rock star dreams. When he'd ended up spending more time bartending and working in restaurants than cutting Platinum records, he'd accrued enough experience to run the restaurant arm of Hotel Kings.

She stepped out of the car and ignored the tickle of anxiety dancing down her spine. Laidback Austin wasn't planning on staying overnight, so there shouldn't be a discussion of crashing at her or Jack's place.

She hoped.

Time for a meeting with the architect and Jack about the restaurant's progress. She hadn't seen much of him this week. Every night she'd study late, and if Jack was awake when she returned, he'd be tucked up in bed with his nose in one of his gory paperbacks. He'd wave and she'd call out good night. All very nonchalant, like they were two polite strangers temporarily rooming together instead of...whatever they were.

The minute she closed the bedroom door behind her, her shoulders would sag. They couldn't keep up the routine for much longer without one of them breaking. Or at least her. He was so casual that she almost questioned whether they'd really hooked up or she'd dreamed it.

"There you are. The architect is ready to roll." Jack stood in front of her, looking sinfully handsome in a white polo-shirt and olive khakis.

She gulped. "Hey, you didn't have to come out and greet me." *Because you are too dangerous to my equilibrium.*

He flashed a playful grin. "Let's rephrase that, shall we? Hi Jack, my favorite person in the world, I'm so happy you're here."

She rolled her eyes and chuckled. "Oh, sorry. That's what I meant to say."

He nodded. "I thought so. Seriously though, I was over on this side of the property and saw you pull up. Let's head back."

She fell into step next to him. "I was on the phone with Austin, and he'll meet you here around ten-thirty tomorrow. I'll catch up with you to discuss some food and beverage specifics over lunch. I've also got a couple wine tastings set up over in Tin City in the afternoon. Sound good?"

He nodded. "Sure. Good, that's good. I'll be done with a video conference on some Beverly Hills negotiations by then."

They crossed through the main outdoor courtyard space leading to where Chez Paul Marc, hopefully one day a Michelin Star restaurant, was under construction. "Do you get tired of swapping back and forth between lawyer and managing director?"

One of Jack's most attractive traits was his razor-sharp mind and his approachability, which made him a smooth negotiator.

"No, it's a pretty easy transition. Different aspects of the business, that's all." He shrugged one broad shoulder. "

"I don't know how you juggle it all." She smiled and shook her head.

"Sheer talent." He flashed his dimple. "You know you don't have to stay out so late, if we can work together during the day, we can have dinner together in the apartment."

Her heart knocked against her ribcage. "I'm not avoiding you. It's easier to lock myself away into a cubicle at the library without any distractions."

He smirked. "You've called me a distraction several times now."

She smacked his shoulder. "Oh please. Remember way back into the olden days when you were in law school and how dry some of the information you had to memorize was. Same with me now and even if you weren't at the condo, I'd go to the library. Otherwise, I'd end up in the bathroom scrubbing the tile with a toothbrush or re-arranging the linen closet to avoid it."

"Hey, I'm only three years older than you, not thirty. I'm teasing you, Campbell, like I've always done." His tone was light.

Had she imagined the most passionate night of her life? Maybe Jack was simply a great compartmentalizer.

She could be, too. Time to stow visions of naked Jack deep into the back section of her brain's vault. *Keep it casual, girl. It's what you wanted.*

When they reached the restaurant, she forced a smile.

"No worries. I'm excited to see what Brad has to say about the design tweaks."

The lanky architect waved at them.

"Let's do this. Do you want to grab dinner afterwards or is it another late library night?" Jack asked, his dark brows raised.

She froze. "Oh, I'm actually meeting Sylvia tonight. We've got some practice tastings to review. But we'll hang with Austin tomorrow, okay?"

His lips tightened for a split second before his expression smoothed out. "Sure." He addressed Brad. "We're ready."

She squared her shoulders and followed him. The architect was one more person she could practice her, "oh we're colleagues and old family friends" act before the real challenge with Austin ensued tomorrow.

Jack wasn't the only one who could maintain a pleasant façade no matter what simmered beneath the surface.

JACK HAD PERFECTED the skill of appearing to be listening intently while doing nothing of the kind. It all started in ROTC where the only way he could cope when a drill sergeant barked orders at him was to tune it out or risk reacting. In law school, a few of the crustier old professors adored him because they assumed his creased brow and penetrating gaze meant he was engrossed with the subject matter. When classes centered on topics like how much corn to store in silos or disputes over easements between agricultural plots––not so much.

Right now, his talent served him well. While it might appear he was part of a discussion on maximizing the wine dinner experience through the strategic placement of high-top and regular tables, if either Campbell or Brad asked him a question, he would be totally busted.

He'd talked a good game earlier about hanging out like she was a colleague and his best friend's little sister. Who the hell was he kidding? Acting cool around Campbell all week had taken a toll. Everything had changed from one night and his chest tightened whenever she was near.

Hell, whenever he thought about her, which was way too often these days. He needed to remain focused on his end goal of proving to himself and his friends he wasn't like his parents. That he wasn't always chasing the next shiny thing on the horizon. Maison du Soleil was his chance to plant roots.

Damn, if circumstances had been different-- they didn't work together, she wasn't Cam's baby sister, and she wasn't possibly moving away--he'd pursue her. Their connection was simply too powerful. Although, those were excuses.

There wasn't a legal barrier to them dating--he hadn't included a no-fraternization clause in the Hotel Kings' employment contracts. In the hospitality world, it would be a practical impossibility. Ryan and Charlie worked together opening Pacific Jewel Inn and were now engaged.

Campbell was an adult and chose who she did or didn't date. Her big brother might not like Jack and Campbell being a couple, but he couldn't stop them if that's what they wanted.

She'd made it clear she was open to leaving Paso for the right opportunity. He was committed to running Maison du Soleil and the Hotel Kings team. He couldn't leave. If he relaxed his guard and allowed himself to fall for her, he'd be vulnerable.

If and when she left, she would break his heart.

CHAPTER 14

Campbell hurried into Les Petites Canailles. Jack and Austin were seated at a table in the back, two handsome dark-haired men deep in conversation. She waved at the hostess and headed directly across the high-ceilinged, bright restaurant to join them. Her heels echoed on the hardwood floor and both guys glanced up before she reached the table.

When Jack's tiger-eyed gaze caught hers, her throat tightened, and her step hitched.

One look from those light green eyes stole her breath.

Austin rose from the table and enveloped her in a hug. "We were about to send out a search party––you're never late. Everything okay?" He stood back and studied her face.

She nodded. "I'm so sorry. Studying."

Campbell slid into the empty chair next to Jack, careful not to get too close. Although his clean masculine scent and the heat from his lean muscular frame was inescapable.

"We were talking about how great everything looks so far at Chez Paul Marc. Now we just need to decide on the chef." Jack turned to her, his baritone casual.

"But first, some wine for the Master Sommelier." Austin filled her wineglass. "I was parched and couldn't wait for you to choose. I know the restaurant owner's father owns L'Aventure but I ordered another one of your favorite Chardonnays."

"Like you aren't an expert. Thank you and yes, I do love the Mount Eden Estate Chardonnay." She sampled the chilled straw-colored liquid. "It's the perfect temperature too. So, Austin, you had some interviews set up for next week, right?"

He nodded and his angular, square-jawed face broke into a grin. "I've got it narrowed down to four great candidates. They all bring different experience to the table so it's going to depend on what feels like the right fit. Any chance you could fly down to San Diego next week?"

Her eyes widened. "No way. Do you think you could narrow it down to two and then arrange for them to come up here? I'm fully booked and next Friday is our wine dinner at Epoch so the whole team, including you, should be in town."

Jack nodded. "I agree they need to come to Paso. Depending on what they're used to, they might think we're too remote a destination. We want to ensure whoever we bring on board views Maison du Soleil and Chez Paul Marc as a long-term commitment."

Campbell stiffened. Jack wasn't making an indirect dig at her with the commitment comment, was he?

Austin raked his fingers through his shoulder-length black hair. He looked more like a sexy rock star than a Food and Beverage Director for a luxury hotel chain. But his slightly rumpled appearance suited him. "That's a great point. I mean, I've made it crystal clear that we want a farm-to-table French influenced restaurant and it's basically on a deserted mountain, miles from town."

"I know we've been clear. But we want someone who will fall in love with this place. Feel connected to it," Campbell said. There was magic sprinkled on the Central Coast that wound around your heart like tendrils of morning fog.

"What she said." Jack grinned and pointed his thumb at her.

"Like you both have. You two are the perfect pair to run this location." Austin reclined back against his chair and glanced between the two of them. "Hell, I love it here but doubt I could be this far away from a major airport long-term."

The hairs on the back of Campbell's neck prickled at Austin's choice of words. Her teenage daydreams certainly cast her and Jack as the perfect couple. But back then she'd been blissfully unaware of the complications of adult life--like career dreams and responsibilities taking precedence over romance.

Jack laughed and leaned forward. "That's part of what I love about it. The SLO or San Jose airports are far enough away to discourage visitors who aren't serious about wine country. The guests we're hoping to attract are looking for a secluded retreat focused on wine, gourmet food, and nature."

Keep the focus on the hotel, girl. Campbell nodded and patted Jack's sinewy forearm then snatched her hand back when sparks singed her fingers.

She smoothed back a strand of hair. "He's right. Paso Robles wants to keep the wine community more intimate and less corporate/commercial. The fact that it's a little more difficult to reach adds to the appeal. We hope."

Austin's eyes narrowed at her theatrical movement but didn't comment. As a musician, he was a natural observer so not a chance he'd missed her awkward hand flap. She avoided his gaze and picked up her wineglass.

Luckily, distraction arrived in the form of a curvy

brunette waitress who placed a massive charcuterie and cheese platter on the mahogany table. "Here you go. Are you all ready to order your main courses yet?"

"Thank you. I'm sorry but I need a little more time. Can you give us a few minutes?" Campbell picked up her menu and scooted away from Jack as far as possible without falling off the seat. Just to be safe.

Jack loaded up his plate with prosciutto di parma, salami, and manchego cheese. "I'm starving. I really need to remember to pick up breakfast or bring some food out to the hotel with me."

"Need me to come stock up your refrigerator for you? We can't have our Managing Director starving to death." Austin chuckled and plucked up a niçoise olive.

Jack stiffened. "No."

"He's fine." Campbell blurted at the exact same moment.

Austin tilted his head, his brow furrowed. "Okaaay...so you're helping our culinary challenged friend out? Bought him some Cap'n Crunch? Or let him come over to your place for breakfast?"

Campbell choked on the piece of cheese she'd sampled. "He's gotten coffee a few times, but he knows how to grocery shop. He's always hungry, like he was as a teenager. Right?"

Jack nodded and stuffed a slice of prosciutto into his mouth.

Campbell picked up her wine and downed a healthy mouthful. "Enough about Jack's eating habits. Let me tell you about the two wineries we're tasting at this afternoon. I want to get your opinion because I'm considering stocking some wines from both at all our hotels."

Austin's gaze was speculative, but he dropped it. "Sounds great to me. So, they're versatile enough for our desert visitors in Palm Springs and the peeps in Monterey? It will definitely simplify our lives to have a few of the same wines at each location."

"Well, of course, most will vary because a Zinfandel or 100% Syrah might not work in the desert during the summer, but I'd like to have some of our mainstays be consistent with our brand of wine expertise. I know the vintners will appreciate it, too."

Jack kept munching while she and Austin geeked out about grapes. They ordered lunch and settled into their normal easy camaraderie.

Campbell's tight shoulders softened, and she was able to relax and tuck away all the stress to deal with later.

JACK TOSSED the remainder of his wine into the silver bucket on the counter of the tasting room. As the designated driver this afternoon, he was only sampling a few sips of Austin and Campbell's favorites.

This afternoon was his first visit to Tin City, and it wouldn't be his last. A unique spot in an industrial park where the creators and the sellers of local wines, craft brews, and spirits set up tasting rooms, it was like a one-stop shop. With more than twenty-five artisans, the experience was totally different than traversing the winding roads between Paso Robles wineries.

While Campbell chatted up the winemaker of their current stop about cases and production and the impact of wildfires on the flavor of the wines, Jack simply drank her in. Her intelligence sparkled in her arctic blue eyes, her passion visible with every gesture of her artistic hands, and her confidence was evident. The vintner conversing with her had stars pinwheeling in his dark eyes, dazzled by all things Campbell Taylor.

Jack's jaw clenched. The dude better not try to hit on her.

"Any particular reason you're staring at Garth like you want to kick his ass?" Austin murmured.

Jack snapped his head to look at his friend. "What?"

Austin tapped him on the shoulder. "Walk with me outside for a second. Campbell's got this covered."

Jack frowned and slid off the stool. Had he really been glaring at the cheesy guy? He was losing it. He slid off the stool.

"Hey Campbell, I'm going to show Jack around Tin City while you two talk wine. Be back in about fifteen."

She gave an absent-minded wave and continued chatting with the drooling Garth.

Austin led them out into the afternoon sunshine. He stood on the broad sidewalk, shading his eyes from the glare, looking like a rock and roll version of his older brother Ryan.

"What's up? Were you getting tired of that guy, too? Man, he just wouldn't shut up."

Austin barked out a laugh. "They were talking wine. It's how she discusses it with everyone. Nothing new. But something's up with you."

Jack arched a brow. "Come again?"

"Look, I know you. I know Campbell. You guys were acting weird at lunch, and you've been watching her like a hawk. What gives?" Austin stopped on the sidewalk and turned toward him, eyebrows raised.

Jack swallowed and sweat prickled on the back of his neck. "Don't know what you're talking about. She's amazing at what she does, and I was admiring that. And that guy is a pain in the ass." *Or, yeah, when she touched my arm at lunch I went hard instantly and I want to kill that guy for flirting with her.*

Austin shook his head. "Look dude, I'm the resident fuck up. The black sheep. The failed musician turned restaurant guy. The one who's on board because my brother is the CEO. But I'm observant as hell and something is different between you two."

Jack drew in a sharp inhale and blew out a breath. No way would he reveal Campbell's and his secret. "We're working together now. If I'm noticing that she's an incredible woman, can you blame me?"

Austin's eyes narrowed. "Does she know you're in love with her?"

Jack stuttered. "In love with her? You're out of your mind. I like Campbell. I've always liked Campbell. She's gorgeous. She's brilliant. She's got an incredible work ethic. She's funny and sweet. She's Cam's little sister, for god's sake."

Austin pointed a finger at him. "Love. Man, you've fallen for her. The chemistry shooting off the two of you is electric. Have you two hooked up?"

Jack's pulse accelerated. "Stop. You're seeing things or maybe you're in romantic-ballad-writing mode. She and I are friends, and we work together. That's it." Shit, if Austin saw it so easily, Cam would be on to them in a heartbeat.

"Look, I'm not going to push you but know it's obvious you're into her, okay? And she leapt like a scalded cat when she touched you at the restaurant, so it isn't one sided. But you're Ryan's right-hand man and if something happens to cause a rift between you two, or if Cam goes into over-protective big brother mode or whatever, it impacts us all."

A flicker of irritation shot up Jack's spine. "When Charlie got to La Jolla, you were hitting on her. Now she and Ryan are engaged. Sure, things got awkward for a while, but it all worked out. There's no reason me and Campbell being involved would cause a rift with Ryan."

"So, you have thought about it." Austin crossed his arms over his chest and smirked.

Jack blew out an exasperated breath. "I'm only trying to

address your irrational fears over nothing." When had Austin gotten so damn tricky?

Austin tapped one finger to his chest, his smirk still in place. "I never thought I'd be the one telling anybody else this, but here I am. You two better figure out your shit. The whole team will be here next week and that includes Cam. If you keep looking at her like she's an ice cream sundae on a hot afternoon, the gig will be up."

No way was Jack admitting anything to Austin. But his friend had a point. If he could get out of the damn apartment and not have to feel her sleeping mere feet away, it would help.

He shook his head. "Don't use that line in a song...too cheesy."

Austin lightly punched his shoulder. "You can call me all the names in the book but cheesy isn't one of them."

"Hey guys, what's the deal? You abandoned me to the most verbose person on the planet." Campbell approached, her arms spread wide.

Jack sneered at Austin. "That's what I said, but he insisted you had it handled. Are we done in there?"

Campbell nodded. "We are. They've got great wine and I think I can negotiate an excellent arrangement but yeah, he could definitely talk."

"Did you see the looks Jack was giving the guy? I thought he was going to tell him to shut up, that's why I took him outside." Austin laughed.

Her eyes widened. "I didn't see that. Jack, he's joking, right?"

Jack glared at Austin––resident fuck-up indeed. Trouble-maker was more like it. "Of course. Austin loves to stir stuff up."

Austin held up both hands, the picture of wounded innocence. "Now, now. A little good-natured teasing never hurt anyone. Shall we head to the next appointment?"

Campbell looked between them for a moment and rolled her eyes. "You two are the worst of the crew. How did I end up with you guys?"

"Hey, I didn't do anything. He started it." Jack pointed at Austin and started walking. Time to change the subject. "Where to now, boss?"

Campbell laughed. "Okay, children. We're heading three doors down. Can I trust you both to behave?"

Jack sniffed. "I always behave."

"Yeah, right. Let's do this." Campbell grinned. "You boys be good. The adult has some work to do."

CHAPTER 15

Jack sat in his makeshift office––the front seat of his SUV if one wanted to be particular––and cursed the abysmal connectivity at the Maison du Soleil property. On one hand, it would be excellent for the guests who had a hard time stepping away from their busy lives and relaxing on vacation. They'd have no choice but to unplug.

But for the business end of things, it was proving to be a royal pain in the ass. There was remote and there was *remote.* He jotted down another note in his planner because he didn't trust his cell signal to save it in his smartphone. He'd check with some of the winery owners and other residents near York Mountain to see if they had any special tricks they'd be willing to share.

So far today, he'd been booted off two video conferences and hadn't been able to reconnect. Not ideal when he was dealing with an argumentative attorney causing problems for Cam's Monterey location. Not to mention attempting to assist Lucas with a few pressing issues he was facing with the Beverly Hills zoning commission. He tossed down his phone onto the passenger seat, a.k.a. his desk, and dropped his head back against the headrest.

He'd have to figure out something before the hotel opened because otherwise managing reservations and actually doing business could prove challenging.

He massaged the bridge of his nose and allowed his eyes to close for a moment. In the week since Austin had called him out, he'd tossed and turned most nights. The lumpy bed and the flat as a pancake pillows would send him to a chiropractor soon if something didn't give. And attempting to sleep with the temptation that was Campbell Taylor a room away was worse than he could have imagined. Just ask his left hand.

Over the last week, they'd progressed from complete avoidance to sharing coffee in the morning and an occasional dinner in the evening. A few days, they'd worked together at the hotel, but they drove separately because she frequently held off-site meetings. Except for the fact he went rock hard around her most of the time, being with her was easy. Natural.

Each day, he learned something new about her. Her dry sense of humor meshed with his perfectly and often they'd catch each other's eyes and not have to say a word. Somehow, her pithy comments and witty observations rendered her even more beautiful.

Each day, he found it more difficult to push his unfamiliar feelings back into the vault. Damn it. His eyes flew open, and he slapped his hand against the steering wheel. Austin hadn't been far from the mark. His heart was more involved than he cared to admit and if he wasn't careful, he would fall in love with her and be totally screwed.

Because at the end of the day, his commitment to the team to stay in Paso couldn't be broken. Not if he was going to prove to himself once and for all that he had what it took to be in it for the long haul. They could never be a couple, for a million reasons, and he needed to accept it.

His phone rang--a technological miracle in and of itself--and his dad's name flashed across the screen. Jack jolted upright, suddenly alert. His parents didn't call often.

"Hey, Dad."

"Jack, how are you doing?" His father's voice sounded no more somber than usual, which was a good sign.

His shoulders relaxed. "I'm good, just working hard to keep the hotel launch on track. What's up with you and Mom?"

"Well, I've got big news. I've accepted my final assignment and we're headed to Hawaii, so we'll be closer to you now."

"Hawaii? That sounds great. How come we never ended up there when I was a kid?" They'd moved every two to three years, depending on his dad's transfers. Hawaii would have been better than a few other spots they'd landed.

"We're both pleased. And we'd like to come see you on the way. This will be the last move before we retire."

He blew out a breath and tamped down on the surge of resentment. Their visits or lack thereof were based on their schedule, never his. The empty seats in the parents' section for college and law school graduation were a testament to their priorities.

"What are your dates?" His jaw tightened--he should be happy that they'd even thought of stopping in, right?

"Not for a few months. We'd like to coordinate with your hotel opening. Is it still New Year's Eve?"

Jack's eyes widened. "That's the plan, assuming everything keeps moving along." Had Ryan or someone sent his parents an invitation?

His dad cleared his throat. "Jack, I'm very proud of what you and your friends are doing. I probably haven't told you that often enough."

Jack held the phone away and gave it a double take. His dad wasn't generous with praise. He'd made no secret of his disappointment when Jack didn't go into the military after ROTC nor at least serve in the Navy JAG Corps instead of civilian law practice.

But Jack hadn't wanted to live the way his parents had, always moving based on orders from above. Not like he hadn't been a nomad since college, but he'd chosen his moves. Deliberate choices to enable him up to settle down and one day have something solid. Something lasting. Or at least that's what he told his friends and himself.

"Jack?"

He shook his head. "Sorry. Umm…thanks."

"Your mom's not home right now but she'll call you later this week. We'll have a more detailed timeline soon."

"Sounds good. I've got a few fires to put out here, so I've got to run. Thanks for calling with your news."

"Of course. See you soon."

Jack set the phone down and stared out the windshield at the bright sunshine filtering through the oak tree branches. The headache brewing behind his eyes kicked in for real now. He gripped the steering wheel and squeezed tight--no pity party, no regrets. It wasn't like he was the only one whose childhood hadn't been white-picket fences.

Moving every few years as an only child had been rough, so, he'd developed his easygoing, everything-is-cool personality young. Cultivating long-term friendships simply didn't happen. He'd liked school and excelled in sports and those outlets were what sustained him until college.

When he got to SDSU and met Ryan, Lucas, and Cameron, he'd found three true brothers. Found his family. Four years in one place was the longest he'd ever lasted anywhere. And because his parents had been stationed in Italy, he'd started spending the holidays with the Taylors.

Christine and Clyde had welcomed him in like he was one of their own.

He winced. How would they feel knowing he and Campbell had slept together? That most of his thoughts were about her and they weren't exactly G-rated? When he'd been learning to meditate, he'd read somewhere that the average person had 60,000 thoughts per day, most of them on a repetitive loop, like an old-fashioned movie reel.

Hell, he could be the poster child for the theory because he had two loops: Campbell and Maison du Soleil. And he needed to minimize the first loop and amplify the second.

"Enough." He smacked the steering wheel again. Time to get his ass in gear and not sit here ruminating like a teenage boy in a John Hughes film.

"Talking to yourself and beating up your car again?" An amused feminine voice asked from the window.

He jumped and turned and there she stood, two feet away, a broad smirk on her gorgeous face. Had he conjured Campbell?

"Sneaking up on poor over-worked executives again?" He quirked a brow.

"Well, my heels crunching across the gravel isn't what I'd called quiet, but you seemed focused on the trees. Bird-watching a new hobby? Or should I say yelling at birds?"

"You're hilarious." Something softened in his chest. "I've been dealing with the pathetic wi-fi out here. Finding a solution for it has officially moved to the top of my to-do list."

"Well, I'm headed to a meeting with Rebecca, the events manager at Epoch. I'll make sure to ask how they've gotten around the issue. We've got to be on the same grid, right?"

"Absolutely. That would be great. Do you have a meeting here today?"

"I wanted to check on things before going to Epoch. I'm

on my way out now." She shook her head, her silvery blonde hair a shimmering curtain over her shoulders.

His gut tightened. What he wouldn't give to wrap it around one hand and hold her still while he plundered her mouth. His fingers dug into his thigh hard enough to bruise. So much for minimizing thoughts of Campbell.

"I'm heading inside for a quick meeting with a few of the sub-contractors. I'll walk with you." He gathered his phone and notebook and stepped out of his Range Rover.

They crossed what would be the main parking lot of Maison du Soleil to her car. The early October sunshine beamed down on the building, living up to its namesake-- House of the Sun. A crisp breeze ensured that the heat didn't overwhelm. It also lifted the floral scent from her silky hair into the air, assaulting his senses. He exhaled hard.

"What do you think of grabbing dinner at Thomas Hill Organics tonight? I really want to check out their wine menu in person," Campbell asked.

Danger. Danger. Campbell. A dimly lit restaurant and wine tasting with only the two of them? Hell, he wanted to pounce on her in broad daylight. *Don't be an idiot. Say no.*

"Sure. After today, I could deal with a relaxing dinner and some good company." *Idiot.*

"Jack, hey man, can you come over here pronto?" One of the stoneworkers yelled from across the courtyard."

Today was going to suck. That was a fact. "One minute," he yelled back.

She patted his shoulder, a friendly gesture, but every muscle in his body leapt to attention anyway. "I'll let you get to it. Meet me at 6?"

"Yeah, I'll see you then." He pivoted and headed to deal with the latest crisis. But his mood felt lighter all of a sudden.

It took all his self-control not to turn and watch her saunter back to her car.

~

CAMPBELL TOOK another sip of ice water, her throat parched from an afternoon where she had talked non-stop. She looked up and caught Jack's approach to the table. He strolled through the crowded restaurant looking like a sleek tiger, his green eyes gleaming in the muted lighting. His long, muscular legs ate up the space, and a smile flashed across his face when he caught her gaze. Every single woman's head and some of the guys, too, turned to watch him. He was beyond compelling.

And damn if she hadn't been daydreaming about how compelling he'd been in bed. She gulped more water to cool down her rapidly escalating imagination. Tonight wasn't about lusting after Jack, but about checking out the popular restaurant's wine collection.

Knowledge was power and she would ensure that she curated a unique list at her restaurant and hotel that nobody else could match.

"Hey gorgeous, is this seat taken?" Jack's whiskey smooth voice purred.

"I was waiting for the best-looking man in town." She waved one hand toward the empty chair at their intimate two-person table.

His white teeth flashed, and he sat. "It's your lucky night."

She laughed. "There are some jealous folks shooting daggers at me right now. I'm glad you could come."

He shook his head. "No, I think it is the other way around. I could really use a drink after today. Tell me we're drinking a bottle, not just tasting?"

She grinned. "Oh, drinking for sure. This is one of my recon dinners. Going in as a regular wine-loving diner and checking out what's on the menu. No discussion or analysis."

"I won't ask you a single question about wine. As long as

you don't ask me anything about zoning or environmental oversight, okay?"

She studied his handsome features, noting the slight pinch around his mouth and deeper creases around his eyes. "We have a deal. In fact, here comes the wine now."

The gangly young waiter expertly opened the bottle and she gestured for him to pour. She'd ordered one of her favorite Zinfandels, so sampling wasn't required.

Once he left, she held her glass up to toast. "Here's to it all settling down one of these days."

His lips quirked. "I can drink to that." He took a deep sip. "That's delicious. And to answer your question, it won't be settling any time soon. Likely not until after launch day. I mean, Ryan said he's still smoothing out all kinds of wrinkles in La Jolla. And it's pretty common for it to take a while for things to fall into place."

"Yeah, that makes sense. For now, it's full blast on all cylinders, right? But it's what we signed up for." She'd never seen him look exhausted before, pensive even. "Anything else going on?"

He set down the glass and met her eyes. "Not really. I'm wiped out. And my dad called today."

Her eyes widened. His parents weren't what one would call overly communicative with their only child. "Everything okay with them?"

He shrugged. "They're fine. He told me they're moving to Hawaii for a final assignment. And they want to come to the opening launch gala."

"Wow, that's great. They've got to be so proud of all you've accomplished." And if they didn't appreciate the incredible career he'd built on his own, they needed to pay closer attention.

"Funny you say that, my dad told me he was proud of me and what we're building with Hotel Kings." He paused and sipped his wine. "I don't remember him telling me that before."

Her heart ached and she reached a hand across the table and caught his. "Jack, I'm so sorry."

His eyes flickered, an uncharacteristic hint of vulnerability in his deceptively easy-going façade. "Sorry, don't mean to bring you down. It was…surprising. Sometimes it felt like your mom and dad cared more about how I was doing than my parents did. They definitely showed up for me."

She ran her tongue around her teeth and for the hundredth time wondered what was wrong with his parents. "Well, it is their loss that they haven't told you more often. Because you are incredible. You're brilliant, you know something about everything, which can actually be kind of annoying. And we both know my parents consider you family." She waved a hand, warming to the topic. "You're a kick-ass lawyer, you are doing a great job with becoming Managing Director of a luxury hotel, and everybody likes you."

His eyes warmed and he turned his hand over and wove his long blunt fingers with hers.

"Why are you such a sweetheart? It makes it even harder…" He broke off, withdrew his hand, and picked up his wineglass.

Her breath caught in her throat and her hand felt cold without the heat of his pressing against it. Was he referring to sharing the condo and acting like they were friends after their night together?

Their smoking hot night together. "Harder?"

His grin was wry. "Look, I know we agreed when you said our night together was a one-time thing. That doesn't make it any easier."

"Any easier?" Her pulse accelerated and a flush of heat rose on her cheeks.

He leaned in and lowered his voice. "It doesn't make it any easier to pretend I'm not rock hard for you every day. That I want you to meet me in the restroom in two minutes, push your skirt up, and fuck you against the wall."

The heat dropped and pooled in her center. And once again, he'd taken her breath away. "Jack."

He straightened in his chair. "Sorry. Campbell, I'm sorry. I--"

She held up one hand. "Don't apologize, because I'd be a liar if I pretended I didn't want to say yes."

He closed his eyes and pinched the bridge of his nose. "How much longer until harvest is over again?"

She exhaled a shaky breath. "Depends, but it could go past the end of October, so potentially another four to six weeks."

He hissed. "And when is your exam?"

"December." Damn it. Her exam. Her priorities. Jack was simply too big of a distraction and conversations like this weakened her resolve.

Would one more time really hurt? Was she expending too much energy fighting off the attraction and would she be better off scratching the itch?

The waiter magically appeared, giving them a much-needed interruption in a discussion steamrolling toward reckless abandon.

Like sex in a public restroom at a restaurant in a small town.

Most likely sex punctuated with screams and moans and mind-blowing orgasms.

She pointed at something on the entrée list without reading it. Intermission time. Jack was too appealing, especially showing the hint of sensitivity he rarely revealed to the world. Despite her best intentions, willpower couldn't prevent the slow slide into falling for him. Hell, she'd had a crush on him forever and the reality of him made her school-girl impression a pale imitation.

The timing sucked. Because she couldn't have it all, could she? Or at least not at the same time. Her dreams required 110% unwavering dedication. She'd always put her ambitions first and her life had seemed on track before Jack arrived.

She couldn't afford to fail her exam again and start the process all over again. Couldn't allow the doubters and the haters like awful Roger to have the last laugh.

And Jack Cassidy wasn't a man you asked to wait for you until you'd achieved your career goals. Not exactly the guy you put on ice until you were ready.

Especially when his suggestion had liquid heat curling in her belly.

Jack's phone vibrated and he frowned when he glanced at the screen. He rose from the table. "It's Ryan and I need to talk to him. I'll be back in a minute."

Campbell slumped against the seat and closed her eyes. They were playing with fire. Neither of them had time for anything other than work, work, work for the next few months. Her brain shouted at her to focus on what was the most important thing in the world to her. Her heart sang Jack's name.

CHAPTER 16

"*P*erfect, so we're all set for Friday." Jack leaned against the exposed brick wall in the hallway next to the restrooms, his mind racing.

Holy crap, had he really propositioned Campbell to bathroom sex? No semblance of self-control or even a filter. He was losing it.

But she hadn't tossed her wine in his face and stormed off.

Which meant…she was into it?

"Yeah, everything is fine. And we're lucky that Jordan invited you guys stay at the winery owner's house on Epoch's property Friday night. The town is at full capacity." He squeezed his eyes shut––if Ryan had any idea what the housing shortage had created.

They said goodbye, Jack stepped into the restroom, and splashed icy water on his face. What he needed to cool down was more of a polar bear plunge in the Arctic. He studiously avoided looking at the walls because his imagination was *that* vivid. Time to return to the table and act like he hadn't been a complete tool. And he'd once considered himself smooth, and charming?

Not so much around Campbell.

When he returned, a platter with the burrata and roasted butternut squash appetizer took up half the tiny table. A physical barrier, thank god.

He sank into his chair. "Ryan and Charlie are meeting us at Maison du Soleil on Friday at 2:30 and everyone else will meet us at Epoch at 5 for the wine-pairing dinner."

Campbell's expression was neutral, the earlier flush on her high cheekbones gone. "I have it on my calendar."

"Oh, Cam may or may not stay overnight depending on how long the dinner goes."

Her almond shaped eyes went round. "You spoke to my brother?"

He waved a hand. "Earlier today. He said he'd make a last-minute call. Although he really wants to do the wine tasting, so he'll stay if he does." If only the winery's house were open more than one night. He'd ask to stay there. too.

Campbell's eyes were on the colorful appetizer while she filled her plate. "We should probably talk about a game plan before we see everyone. I'm concerned." She lifted her cerulean gaze, a small crease between her brows.

"Concerned?"

She picked up the white cloth napkin and dabbed the corners of her full pink mouth. "Well, neither of us is sleeping well. Both of us are stressed out. Ryan's the CEO and he and Charlie are both astute. They're going to sense the tension between us, and we need to make sure we're on the same page about what we say."

The cords on the back of his neck tightened. "If this is about what I said--"

She held up a slender hand. "Hear me out. We're both on edge, which isn't good for either of our careers. I'm trying to approach this logically and reasonably and I think I've got a solution."

"A logical, reasonable solution to wanting to tear each other's clothes off?" His lips twitched.

A pink flush stained her cheeks again. She bit her lip and nodded.

He extended one hand, gesturing for her to continue. No idea what was coming next.

"We have to agree and then we need to promise that this is it." Her voice was throaty. Breathless.

He tilted his head. "This is it?"

She gripped the table with both hands and leaned in. "We can't have sex in the bathroom here but I'm afraid if we don't do something tonight, we're going to ruin everything we're working toward. You obviously can't get it out of your head, and neither can I." Her pupils expanded.

All his blood rushed straight south. Maybe he nodded. Maybe he drooled.

"One more night. Tonight." Her lips parted. "But that's it. Get it out of our system before everybody gets here."

He blinked. Blinked again. She was serious. "Campbell." He searched for the words. The right words—*no, your brother, our careers, our plan*—but they wouldn't come.

Rule One in negotiations—whoever speaks first loses.

Fuck it. If this was losing, he'd take it.

"Let's get out of here. I'll tell the waitress to box up our dinner." He shot out of his chair and sprinted to the server station. If they didn't get out of the restaurant stat, he'd explode.

Time to break every speed limit returning to the condo.

~

THEY SPRINTED out and the second they reached his SUV, Jack thrust her up against the passenger door and slanted his mouth against hers. She moaned, plastered her tight little body against his, and dug her fingernails into his hair. He fumbled with the key fob, eager to get home. Or hell, climb into the back seat.

"You are so fucking hot. If it were darker in this parking lot, I would take you up against this car right now," he growled.

Campbell rocked her hips against his hard-on and nipped his lower lip. "Home. Now. Drive fast."

They tumbled into his car, and he stomped on the gas, desperate now. She brushed her fingertips across his chest, trailed them down his abs, then pressed one hand against his aching cock.

His vision blurred and he sucked in a sharp inhale. "I can't see straight when you do that. Stop or we won't make it home."

She purred and slid her hand up to tease the edge of his waistband. "Hurry, hurry, hurry," she sang.

He accelerated into the parking space in front of their building and they leapt from the car. He caught her hand, wrenched the door open, and they burst inside. She kicked the door shut behind them.

"Now. Here. Condom. Clothes." Her tone was urgent, demanding.

She whipped her dress over her head, revealing pale limbs and a scrap of peacock blue lace. He growled and tore his shirt off while her busy hands unbuckled his belt. He grabbed the condom packet from his wallet and together they shoved his jeans down.

Thrusting one hand into her hair, he captured her mouth and backed her up against the wall. He reached between them and cupped her, groaned at how hot and wet and ready she was for him. He plunged two fingers inside her and lowered his mouth to capture one taut nipple.

A slick film of perspiration covered her satin skin, and she rode his hand, her hips rocking against him. Her body vibrated and quaked.

"Please. Now." Her voice was husky, throaty, so damn sexy.

"Please what?" He murmured against her breast, shifting his mouth to give attention to her other breast, lightly raking her with his teeth. Her back arched.

"Fuck me against the wall, Jack. Now." She dug her fingers into his shoulders, leapt up and wrapped her strong legs around his hips.

"When you ask so nicely." He managed through gritted teeth. "I'm going to make you come so hard."

He gripped her hips and entered her in one perfect stroke. She screamed and he slanted his mouth against hers, their tongues swirling and stroking as he pounded into her. Tremors increased through her body, and she came apart, every muscle clenching before she melted in his arms. Unable to slow the tingling in his lower back, he increased his pace, cried out her name, and shattered.

Lights sparked behind his eyes and his knees buckled. Holding her tight, he slid to the floor, rolling onto his back to protect her from hitting the ground. She sprawled on top of him, both of them wheezing like they'd scaled Mt. Whitney.

As their breath began to regulate, sensations began to filter in. The sweet scent of her skin, the tickle of her damp curtain of hair against his shoulders and arms, the silence surrounding them, the discomfort of the hardwood against his spine.

She shifted back, resting her forearms on his chest and met his gaze. "Wow."

"Yeah, wow." His lips curved up.

She lowered her mouth to his in a sweet kiss. "I'm crushing you, aren't I?"

He laughed, amazed that she could joke after the ferocious mating they'd just shared. "Well, now you mention it…"

She giggled and pressed to her feet, in all her naked glory. "Your pants are around your ankles and your shoes are still on."

He sat up. "Someone made me risk a reckless driver ticket, so I didn't dare waste an extra second."

"Oh, I'm definitely not complaining. And I'll be right back." She sauntered toward the bathroom and called back over one creamy shoulder. "I'm starving. Will you get the food out of your truck, please?"

With that sassy comment, Campbell Taylor knocked through another layer of his heart. He'd never experienced anyone like her. They'd practically burned the paint off the wall with rough, raw sex. In the next moment, she could make him laugh.

He dropped his head in his hands, his heart a steady drumbeat in his temples. Having her in his arms was as natural as breathing. She elicited a possessive streak in him that he hadn't known existed. When he'd shared a vulnerable moment about his dad with her, she'd been sympathetic and understanding.

Their history of friendship and shared family added a layer to their connection that was grounded in trust. In security. Yet nothing about their situation approached security.

Despite the shitshow that surrounded them, their bond was undeniable. Austin had been correct––he was in love with Campbell. Good thing he was still on the floor because a wave of light-headedness assaulted him.

And he couldn't do a damn thing about it because she'd made it clear what her priorities were, and he respected her too much to try to sway her. Not that he had a clue as to whether she felt the same or if their explosive chemistry was all that had driven her tonight. Wouldn't that be ironic? Fun-loving, easygoing, no desire to commit Jack Cassidy had finally fallen in love and he couldn't declare his feelings. Couldn't tell anyone.

"Why are you still sitting on the floor? Are you okay?" Campbell rushed over and crouched down beside him, a bottle of ibuprofen in one hand.

She'd swept her hair back into a messy ponytail and washed her face. She wore a faded burgundy Université de Paris sweatshirt and a miniscule pair of shorts that high-lighted her long, toned legs.

He lifted his head and studied her face. "I'm fine. And you are the most magnificent woman I've ever seen. But what's up with the pills?"

She blushed and her thick fringe of eyelashes fluttered down. "Stop."

He shifted forward and cupped her face. "You are. You're such a shining light––inside and out. But are you okay?"

Her eyes gleamed and she pressed a quick kiss on his lips. "Um, that wall was a little hard on my back, not a big deal. And you are delirious from sex and starvation. Let's heat up our dinner. It's still early and I can't have you fainting on me."

She stood and held out one hand. He caught it and rose to his feet. She wanted to keep it light between them. Fun. He could do that for her, but something tugged in his chest. Hell, he'd had a lifetime of acting like he was always fine, and he would damn well do it now.

He flashed a self-deprecating grin. "Maybe you're right about being delirious. But you're beautiful. Be right back. And I'll make sure to give you a thorough back massage to make up for the wall." He yanked his jeans up over his hips but left them unbuttoned and headed to the bedroom to change.

He grabbed his favorite pair of board shorts and a navy Henley. They'd share dinner together, some wine, and if he was lucky, they'd share her bed tonight.

If tonight was all Campbell could offer him, he'd accept.

CHAPTER 17

Campbell double-checked her reflection in the mirror. Not only did she need to be a veritable encyclopedia of wine-related information, she had to have a polished appearance, impeccable social skills, and an ability to upsell and close deals without appearing to sell at all.

No pressure.

Over the last decade, she'd been asked everything from questions about how climate change was impacting winegrower's harvest-time decisions to how Bordeaux wines from 2010 had been impacted by the volcano eruption in Iceland. She had to be able to respond with specific details and relay the information with utter confidence.

No pressure.

She smoothed back her hair she'd styled into a sleek, low ponytail and added her excellent faux-diamond stud earrings. With a forest green wrap dress and a matte burgundy lip, she looked sophisticated and a little bit serious. Maybe it was her imagination, but her mouth looked puffy from last night's kissing and lovemaking. But her eyes gleamed bright because she'd slept like a baby for the first time in weeks.

Wrapped up in Jack's powerful arms.

And like the first time they'd shared a bed, she'd fallen into a deep, dreamless sleep without tossing or turning. So, their ability to sleep curled up like two pieces of a puzzle hadn't been a fluke. It was a fact. One she wasn't going to admit because once she fell down that rabbit hole, she'd have to admit all kinds of things she'd rather not deal with now.

Like the fact she was falling for Jack, for real. No schoolgirl crush. Real love--all the like, respect, infatuation, and years-long feelings all coalesced into one undeniable emotion. Since he'd arrived in Paso, he'd revealed layers of his personality she'd suspected were there but he'd hidden beneath the handsome charming package. His vulnerability about feeling abandoned by his parents, his concern for her well-being, his hint of a quick temper that he never allowed to surface.

This morning they'd foregone any type of discussion of last night and no mention of how to act during today's meeting with the rest of the team. They'd worked from the condo together, an easy camaraderie between them. They'd bargained for one more night yesterday--*well done, me*--and it had to suffice.

Back to reality. Today was jam-packed with work. Both of them knew how to be professional and she'd make damn sure her brother didn't sniff even the teeniest hint of impropriety. She stretched her arms overhead and her lips curved up. If her thighs were sore and she had some stubble burns beneath her conservative dress, it was her secret. And after the toe-curling back massage he'd given her, her back felt better than it had in years. Her gamble had paid off.

She was okay with keeping their affair secret. But her heart yearned to be able to share her feelings with Jack.

While she didn't think he was a player like her brother seemed to, she didn't believe he was looking for a relationship. And hadn't she made it crystal clear she wasn't committing to Paso once she'd completed her Master Sommelier status?

Hell, she could technically be the Beverage Manager from any of the Hotel Kings locations, but she loved being in wine country. If she and Jack were in different places in their life and decided to see each other, Cam would have to deal with it. But they weren't. Paso had burrowed beneath her skin. But if a Michelin star restaurant in Paris or Rome called, would she be a fool to turn it down? She couldn't know until it actually happened.

"Hey, are we driving separately or together?" Jack called from the living room.

With one final glance in the mirror, Campbell strode out of the bedroom on camel-colored stilettos. "Let's go together. No need to take two cars, right?" They'd already had to fetch her car from the restaurant this morning.

Jack's eyes hooded. "I don't know, we're back to being friends and colleagues today but you look good enough to eat."

Her breath quickened and a flare of heat shot through her belly at the memory of his talented mouth nibbling and tasting every inch of her. "Jack. You can't say things like that."

He facepalmed and had the grace to look mildly abashed. "I'm sorry. You're right. We agreed. I'll do better."

She shook her head and glanced down at her watch. "We're meeting Ryan and Charlie in an hour and then everybody, including Cam, will be at Epoch later. I can't do this by myself."

He set down his coffee mug on the quartz countertop and approached her on those long muscular legs. "By the time we see them, I'll be the supreme professional. But before we go, can I say one last thing?"

She held her breath and nodded. Maybe if his sharp, clean scent didn't assault her senses she'd be able to keep her composure. But damn, with a crisp white button-down highlighting his handsome face, the struggle was real.

He stopped about an arm's length from her and reached for her hands. He linked his warm fingers with hers and his crystalline jade eyes deepened. "Last night was special. You are special. I know your career is your priority and I respect that. I respect you. We've both got a lot on our plates. But if circumstances were different, I would do everything in my power to be with you."

Her breath lodged in her throat. "Be with me?"

"Be with you in every way a man and a woman can be together. But we both know the timing isn't right. So, I'll stand back and be your friend and partner and we'll open this hotel, and you'll fulfill your dreams of becoming a Master Som, wherever that takes you. I'll be right here in Paso." His grip tightened.

Every nerve ending in her body crackled and her heart crashed against her ribs. "I--"

He gave a small shake of his head. "I'm not telling you this looking for a response or asking you for anything. But I couldn't keep it inside, not now."

She exhaled an unsteady breath and stepped into his embrace, hugging his lean waist. His arms banded about her. She rested her cheek against his firm chest and the steady beat of his heart filled her senses. The man she'd dreamt of for years wanted her and circumstances were against them.

"Oh Jack, I wish things were different. Because I wish I could say let's see where this goes, but I know myself and I've got to stay on track for my exams."

He stroked his palm down her back. "I know. I won't stand in your way, and I won't bring this up again."

The alarm on her phone sounded, indicating it was time to go to Maison du Soleil. She managed a laugh, despite the tangle of emotions flooding through her. "See, I need to set alarms throughout the day to make sure I'm on time."

He stepped back, his expression neutral. "We all know how Ryan gets if anybody is thirty seconds late."

She smiled, then turned to pick up her satchel. "Cam always said he thought Ryan would have made an incredible soldier if he'd chosen to go active duty instead of into the Army Reserve with the rest of you."

"Hey, he didn't say that about me?" Jack's lips twitched.

She snorted. "I think his exact words, which you should remember, were 'Jack would be too busy trying to schmooze the officers to negotiate better accommodations, tastier food, and more leave.'"

"Yeah, pretty much. Well, here we are. I'm in charge of one of the hotels and so is your brother. We took different paths, but we've ended up in the same role." He frowned.

"You're stuck with the Taylors." She injected a note of false cheer in her tone. "Oh, and I forgot to mention my mom called yesterday to remind us they're hosting Thanksgiving at their new place in Pacific Grove, and you're expected to be there."

He winced. "Well, that's more than a month away. I'll be in my own place by then, so we'll have some distance between us."

A weight settled on her heart. Life wasn't fair. But she needed to suck it up and focus on today. Day by day. She'd been the one who pushed him last night and she'd stick to her promise of moving forward. Although every moment she spent with Jack was one more vine wrapping around her heart.

"Okay, colleagues and old friends, starting now. You're okay driving, right?"

He nodded. "Sure. Let's get going so we beat Ryan and Charlie to the hotel. I don't want to hear him give me any crap since he basically lived at Pacific Jewel during the renovations."

"Deal. And if there happened to be a finished carriage house next to the rear entrance of Maison du Soleil, we all know you'd be there, too." And perhaps her heart would still be intact.

He laughed. "Absolutely. I want to run some numbers by you on the drive up to make sure they're in line with what you've got for food and beverage so far."

He unlocked the doors of his Range Rover. Heat rose in Campbell's cheeks––the last time she'd heard that click and beep, they were falling into his car in their hurry to tear each other's clothes off. She took a few cleansing breaths and hurried to the passenger door.

Time to drag her focus away from mind-blowing orgasms with the man of her dreams and concentrate on manifesting her dreams of being the best Beverage Director for Hotel Kings, LLC and Master Sommelier Extraordinaire.

JACK COMMENDED himself on his superhuman ability to compartmentalize their discussion from the condo and discuss balance sheets and estimated revenue with Campbell. An inner voice was yelling at him for basically spilling his guts to Campbell. But he hadn't been able to shut himself up. And now he was realizing sharing those feelings with her had been selfish on his part. Not his intention, but selfish, nonetheless.

He couldn't lie to himself. Part of him hoped that after

last night she'd want to date him and see where things went. Part of him hoped she'd reciprocate and throw caution to the wind and say she'd stay in Paso Robles once she'd achieved Master Sommelier. That she'd love her role with Hotel Kings enough to stay here, too. That she could follow her dreams here. With him…

Selfish bastard.

And she hadn't said a word about the present or the future.

"I think we beat Ryan and Charlie here, thank goodness," Campbell said as he parked the car beneath the shade of his favorite oak tree.

He surveyed what would be the formal parking lot for the hotel and confirmed it contained only workers' trucks and not Ryan's black BMW. He and Charlie were driving up from La Jolla because they were also going to Monterey to work with Cam.

"Perfect. If we hurry, we can pretend we've been here since dawn slaving away." Time to keep their interactions casual and eliminate the undercurrents.

She laughed, like he'd intended. "Sounds like a plan. I also need to ask Brian if he's gotten any updates on the garden. I want the chef candidates to be able to see where their fresh vegetables and herbs will grow."

His nostrils flared––Brian would be thrilled to see Campbell again. He forced his voice to sound casual. "Great idea. And the design with such enormous windows in the kitchen is unusual."

She nodded. "Exactly, the views of the hills and sky are incredible. This environment will attract a certain type of personality. No dark cramped kitchen here."

He turned to her as they crossed to the wide-open entrance. "Yeah, the real test will be when the contenders visit. I think this place either calls to you or it doesn't."

York Mountain had gotten in his blood. When the hotel was finished and running smoothly, he'd find a house or build a house as close to it as possible. Even the banging, drilling, and shouting from the construction crew couldn't dispel the sense of calm that permeated this land.

"Jack! Campbell! Wait up." Charlie's raised voice reached them over the din.

They stopped and waited for the CEO and Vice President of Sales and Marketing to join them. Despite the rutted, gravel driveway, he hadn't heard their car. The two blonds striding toward them looked more like actors who would play hotel executives on a night-time soap opera. Ryan, who had devoted his entire career to becoming the ultimate hotel industry expert, was the mastermind behind Hotel Kings. Charlie, the woman who'd stolen his friend's heart, was just as savvy.

It had been a blast watching the vivacious Charlie Ray soften up the serious and intense Ryan, his brother from another mother. He glanced at Campbell and a hint of envy for what Ryan and Charlie shared pulled at him.

Campbell tapped her watch with one finger and called out, "I was getting worried, there's only forty-two seconds until our appointment."

"He was white-knuckling it like a ninety-year-old out for a Sunday drive." Charlie smirked and shoulder bumped her fiancé.

"You're all hilarious. I forgot how winding these roads are back here. We should have been here ten minutes ago," Ryan said with a grimace.

"It's perfect. People have to start slowing down before they arrive on the property. Part of the Maison du Soleil experience." Jack waved one arm dramatically toward the work-in-progress.

Charlie nodded. "That's an excellent point. I'm putting

some finishing touches on the marketing materials and may incorporate something about how the escape begins the moment you turn off Highway 46."

Together, they headed into would soon be the LEED Platinum Certified hotel, where the marriage of luxury and eco-consciousness would become the ultimate retreat for wine lovers from around the world.

"This place is going to be one of a kind. Awesome job, you guys." Ryan checked everything out as they made their way to the rear portion of the hotel where Brian waited with the current progress reports. They'd review everything from the solar energy panels to the glass work, the flooring, the gardens, and the low flow water fixtures and drip irrigation for the landscaping.

Campbell nodded enthusiastically. "Jack is doing such an incredible job. The contractors and tradespeople adore him and jump whenever he requests anything. This will be the smoothest hotel opening of the entire chain, I know it."

Jack hadn't blushed since junior high, when he'd asked out a ninth grader who had laughed in his skinny, gawky face. Heat rose on the back of his neck.

"She's exaggerating. You should see the miracles she convinced Brian to do to adjust the footprint of the restaurant so it's perfect." Because Brian would jump off the roof to impress her. Not that Jack would mind.

A crease appeared between Charlie's eyebrows. "Aren't you two the mutual admiration society?"

Ryan paused, a speculative glint in his eye. "See, sweetie, this is what it looks like when two people opening a hotel get along. Isn't it refreshing?"

Charlie burst out laughing. "Don't be bitter because you were the rudest man on earth after *you* hired *me*. It all worked out at Pacific Jewel despite your behavior."

"My behavior? You're the one--"

Campbell avoided Jack's gaze. "You two crack me up. I thought the bickering would die down now you've set a wedding date."

Charlie pressed a kiss to Ryan's cheek. "It's all in fun. He's so easy to tease."

Ryan's jaw softened and his lips twitched.

Jack cleared his throat. "Now now. No time for foreplay, we have work to do." Thank god they'd gotten side-tracked. Ryan had looked curious and when Ryan Michaels wanted answers, he didn't stop digging until he was satisfied. No need to question how well he and Campbell got along.

Time to redirect all discussions to the hotel. Ryan, as CEO, was laser-focused on the bottom line and Jack would keep the afternoon centered on a successful launch. Once the whole group met up at Epoch's Tasting Room, the attention would be on wine and food and catching up.

He'd avoid Campbell and her big brother all night.

Easy, right?

CHAPTER 18

Campbell needed a moment. She excused herself from Epoch Winery's private room, where Rebecca, the charming events manager, held court and entertained the Hotel Kings with her knowledge and humor. Jordan Fiorentini, Epoch's head winemaker, had agreed to collaborate on one-of-a-kind tastings and educational events at Maison du Soleil to cater to wine lovers from around the globe. Tonight was a test run.

Campbell surveyed the long table, satisfied the team remained engrossed in the pre-dinner wine tasting. She couldn't help but admire the environmentally sustainable unique space that blended into nature. From the original redwood used for posts and beams to the concrete floor and natural stone walls, every inch of the rustic yet modern winery was breathtaking.

"Campbell, wait up," Charlie called and rose from the table laden with bottles and wineglasses.

As V.P. of Sales and Marketing, Charlie coordinated the sales and marketing for all the Hotel Kings' properties. Campbell hadn't spent a lot of time with Charlie, but they'd clicked immediately. She was clever, bubbly, and a total sweetheart.

Campbell paused at the floor-to-ceiling glass doors. "You want to come with me to the bathroom and tell me what you think of Epoch and the hotel and Paso so far?"

Charlie linked an arm through hers and they crossed the vast, high-beamed ceiling main area. "I love this place. The GSM blends we've tasted so far are divine and you said we'll be digging into some Reserve wines at dinner, right?"

"Oh good. And absolutely we are."

They entered the modern restrooms and freshened their lipstick at the wide concrete sinks. Part of Charlie's charm was her ability to disarm you with her genuine warmth and interest in whatever you were discussing. Ryan was a lucky guy.

"Before they notice we're gone, we've got to go outside for a minute because I've got something to show you." She couldn't wait to surprise Charlie.

"Ooh, intriguing." Charlie's unusual onyx eyes widened.

"I know Rebecca can handle any of their wine questions for a few minutes, but let's hurry." They crossed to another set of enormous glass doors leading to an enormous patio overlooking vast golden fields.

Charlie's face reflected her awe. "Wow, these views are incredible. Ryan told me the hotel is going for a similar vibe with the repurposed wood and materials. I love it. So peaceful."

"We modeled some of the plans after Epoch's––the design will help keep the buildings naturally cool. But that's not what I wanted to show you. I see Corky now, so follow me." She started down the stairs toward the gigantic horse barn and paused in the field of tall grasses.

"Corky?" Charlie followed her.

"Here he is." She stopped in front of the fluffy brown

Maine Coon. Jack had mentioned that Charlie rescued two feral kittens in La Jolla and loved cats.

"Oh my god, he's adorable." Charlie crouched down and the cat strolled right up and rubbed against her. "And he's a Hemingway cat."

"A Hemingway cat?"

"He's got six toes, which is called a polydactyl or a Hemingway cat for the ones he had in Key West. Oh my, what a cutie. And he lives here?"

She nodded. "Yeah, and there's another one, a big gray boy named Levi. But Corky has been here longer. They basically run the place."

Charlie stood and dusted the fur off her cranberry-colored jumpsuit. "This is already my favorite new winery but the cats clinch it. And the hotel is going to be one of a kind. You're so lucky you get to live here in Paso and work with Jack. I adore him."

Her breath caught in her throat. Lucky was one word for it. "Jack's always been great. We're both putting in a lot of hours." Deflect. Divert. Minimize any fibs. "What about you and Ryan? I know you've set the wedding for May at Cypress Coach Ranch."

Charlie beamed. "Working and living together works surprisingly well for us. Who would have thought? And I can't wait to drive up to Monterey tomorrow and see the progress."

Something tightened in Campbell's chest. Envy perhaps? "You guys are really lucky to do both. We should get back or they'll send out a search party."

Charlie rolled her eyes. "Or drink all the wine."

She cracked up. "Or that. Which would be worse."

They returned to the wine room, where it appeared nobody had noticed their absence. Everyone had come up to central California––Ryan and Charlie and their assistant Jon,

Austin, Lucas, and Cam. She hadn't seen everyone together since the opening launch of Pacific Jewel Inn on Labor Day weekend.

Jack glanced up and snared her gaze, his green eyes hot. He quickly shuttered his expression. Austin sat directly across from Jack and turned toward her, a speculative glint in his eyes.

Had he noticed Jack's expression? *Damn it.*

"There you two are; we need your superior palates and knowledge. Campbell, try to explain a few things to these two hopeless beer drinkers." Austin pointed at Cam and Lucas.

"I've been doing an excellent job, but nobody listens to me." Jon sniffed.

"I appreciate wine." Lucas, a ginger-haired dead ringer for the guy on Outlander elbowed Austin. "He's trying to quiz me about things nobody but a bloodhound or a sommelier could distinguish."

Cam smirked at Austin. "My sister knows more than you. And yeah, I like beer better. I like these wines, especially the 2018 Block B. I don't have to recite every tasting note."

Campbell wagged a finger at Austin--deflect and divert. "How many times have I told you not to quiz the guests? If everyone here were paying guests, we wouldn't want it to feel like they were taking an academic class on wine. Depending upon the specific demographic, the goal is to slip in some knowledge as part of the experience."

Austin winked and returned to a lively conversation with Lucas and Jon. Jack, Charlie, and Ryan were huddled together sniffing their new pours and chatting with Rebecca, the fiery redhead.

She walked over to her brother and massaged his shoulder. "And don't you have excellent taste, big brother. Block B is the beloved wine of many a high-end wine buyer." He angled his head up and studied her expression.

"Maybe I have a palate like yours but it's more suited to beer. But I do appreciate a full-bodied red wine." He shrugged one shoulder.

She settled into the empty seat next to him. "Makes sense." She sipped her wine and closed her eyes in appreciation. "Wow, that's good."

He chuckled. "Get that word out of your vocabulary before your exam."

"Ha ha. I was planning on standing up and declaring that I love wine because it's a pretty color and tastes yummy. Do you think I'll pass with that?" Although she smiled, her gut twisted recalling her initial failure.

"With that brain of yours and the Taylor palate, you can do whatever you want." He studied her expression. "But something's up. What's wrong?"

She sucked in a sharp inhale. Her brother knew her too well. "I'm a little stressed about taking the exam again. I've never failed a test before, and it rattled me."

His blond eyebrows, so like her own, drew together over his long, straight nose. "You said almost nobody passes it on the first try, right?"

"True. But between how busy I am with the hotel and study group and everything, I'm stressed out." She dropped her gaze and swirled the ruby liquid in her glass.

"Are you dating?"

She froze. "What?"

His glacial blue eyes narrowed. "I asked if you're dating anyone?"

She pressed her hand to her throat. "Oh, no. No time for dating." Holy crap, she'd automatically assumed he'd referred to dating Jack.

"Mom and Dad will get on you at Thanksgiving about it. Balance and all that."

"Pot. Kettle. Black. Yeah, Camille really needs to get married so you and I can focus on the hotels. Because I've got no time for relationships until after I pass my exams next year." *Despite having the most tempting man in the world sleeping mere feet from me.*

Despite the fact Jack was her dream man. But despite all the pretty words he'd told her earlier, he didn't have a great track record of sticking around. And Campbell couldn't gamble with her career. Not at this point.

He rubbed his jaw, his eyes flat. "Yeah, we'll have to make them focus on Camille, although that guy's a tool."

It wasn't the first time she'd seen a bleak expression settle over his features. She placed one hand on his forearm and lowered her voice. "Are you okay? Really okay?"

He met her gaze, his eyes like looking in a mirror. "Most of the time. Sometimes the leg bugs the hell out of me, and sometimes it's hard to stop the nightmares. I manage, though."

Her heart ached for her brother. The lower half of his left leg was a state-of-the-art prosthetic, and his limp was minimal, but for a guy who had been in prime shape his entire life, having to cope with physical limitations was tough. As for his mental health? It was her primary concern. He'd never been effusive, but he'd grown more reserved since his return.

They'd been close growing up and he confided in her more than anyone, but he hadn't shared much in the last year. It wasn't healthy. An idea began to gel.

"Well, I was planning to get up to Monterey sooner than later to meet with some food and beverage candidates and the wedding planner Charlie's planning on hiring. She wanted me to back up her choice. If I came up next week, could I stay with you?"

He smacked his glass onto the table. "Like I told Mom and Dad, I don't need a babysitter."

She winced. "Look, don't be so defensive. We all love you. But this is more about me. I'm having a hard time concentrating here right now. Everything with the hotel's restaurant and wine cave is on track and I can do my other work from anywhere. It would help me out."

He studied her, his eyebrows raised. "Why can't you focus here? Is Jack a distraction?"

She gasped. "Jack? How?" Oh my god if he had any idea.

"Look he's one of my best friends. He's a damn brother to me. But he's different than you and me. He can socialize all night and work all day and always bounces back. You and I have never been good at juggling work and play. If he's been pushing you to entertain clients or work too late, just tell me."

A flash of irritation surged through her, and she shifted back in her chair. "Are you kidding me? Jack has an incredible work ethic and isn't partying. And if I don't want to do something, I know how to say no." *For god's sake.*

He held up both hands at her fulminating glare. "I'm not ripping on him. Hell, I've always been jealous how he makes it all look so easy. I'm just trying to figure out why you want to leave town."

She crossed her arms over her chest and gripped her upper arms. "Fine. But that's not why." Now that her plan had coalesced, she'd pull out all the stops because she needed to make sure her brother was okay. It was the perfect solution. At least for a week or two.

"Like I said, the hotel's super busy and I find myself jumping in to help in other areas. I can't afford to do that right now, with the test coming up in December. If I tell my mentor I need to be in Monterey for work, he'll understand. You'd be helping to preserve your little sister's sanity." And create some much needed space between her and Jack.

Her brother's history of over-protectiveness dated back to grade school, when she'd been bullied by a group of older girls. Ever since, if he sniffed out any perceived threat, he'd jump in to save the day. He wouldn't be able to resist helping her.

If a small twinge of guilt ran through her, she allayed it with the fact she'd be able to observe Cam for a few days and create the break she and Jack needed to go back to being friendly colleagues. It was worth a try.

"Fine. But if this is some wild plot to babysit me, you're coming back here." His jaw tightened.

She rolled her eyes. "Yeah, like anyone could ever babysit you. Okay, I'll come up Sunday night. Thanks."

"Don't push it." His lips twitched and her heart warmed to see his sense of humor, which hadn't been evident like it used to before the Middle East, surface.

"Don't push what?" Jon asked, his perfectly groomed eyebrows raised. "What are you two Taylors plotting over there?"

Campbell rose from her chair and waggled her eyebrows. "World domination. If you ever get tired of La Jolla, come work up here with us."

Jon smirked. "Oh, Pacific Jewel would fall apart without me. You know Charlie and Ryan would burn down the place without me playing mediator."

"You crack me up." Charlie laughed. "Will you help me wrap things up and make sure we're prepared for the wine-pairing dinner? Jordan should be here soon and she's going to be giving us the experience of a lifetime."

Jon clapped his hands. "Everybody get up and make sure

you've made notes on the wines and have questions prepared. Meet back in here in thirty. Chop-chop."

"Did you say Jordan draws visual tasting notes for all the wines? Do we get to see those?" Lucas asked.

Campbell nodded. "Yes, in addition to her engineering and Italian degree, she also studied Art, so she creates vinpressions to express the texture of the wines. We should be able to take a peek tonight."

"That's so cool," he said. "Maybe I can lure her down to Beverly Hills when it's time to open my hotel."

"Definitely ask her. Okay, let's do this." The rest of the group stood, and Campbell hurried to help Rebecca clear the table to prepare for the wine dinner.

"I'm going to take Ryan to see Corky and hopefully Levi. We'll be back in a few." Charlie called over her shoulder. She and Ryan strolled toward the vast patio.

Jack laughed. "Whoever would have thought Ryan would turn out to be such a cat lover."

The corner of Cam's mouth lifted. "Right? Being with Charlie has definitely softened him up."

She rested a hand on her hip. "I think they bring out the best in each other and what's wrong with that, you cynical old bachelors?"

Jack's expression sobered. "Nothing is wrong with that. I think they're damn lucky."

Cam merely grunted.

Campbell rolled her shoulders back. Time to enjoy the rest of the evening and attempt not to stress over telling Jack she was leaving.

It was for the best. For both of them.

$\mathcal{J}$ack unlocked the front door to their--scratch that--the front door to *Campbell's* condo. They entered and he tossed the keys on the kitchen island and rubbed the back of his neck, which felt more like iron ridges than muscles. Somehow, they had survived the day and evening without anyone noticing their relationship had changed.

Hell, who was he kidding? Everything had changed.

Thank god the rest of the crew was heading up to Monterey tomorrow because the strain of not looking at Campbell, of sitting far away from her at the dinner, of not touching her on the drive home, had strained the bounds of his self-control.

They hadn't spoken much in the car, but they'd blasted some classic Fleetwood Mac tunes, which always made him nostalgic for time with the Taylors. Mrs. T was a die-hard Stevie Nicks fan.

"I think tonight went really well, don't you?" Campbell threw herself onto the couch and propped her feet up on the low-coffee table. She'd slipped off her stilettos and even her feet were pretty, with their scarlet toenails.

He gripped the cool quartz countertop, keeping his distance. "It was incredible. You were right about Epoch and Jordan. It's going to be a really fruitful partnership."

She slid the band out of her hair and her shiny blonde hair cascaded around her shoulders. "I'm really excited about it. And thanks again for being the designated driver––you missed some exceptional wines. But lucky for you, I brought a 2018 home and I think we should have a glass, even though it's a little young."

No need to admit the sobriety helped him keep his guard up. But now they were home, the strain of the day weighed on him. A glass of special wine would be just the ticket. "You're the expert. Want me to pour?"

She gazed up at him and nodded. "It's in my bag. My feet are killing me so that would be lovely."

He grabbed the wine and admired the 2018 Epoch Estate Blend bottle, with its plum and fuchsia label. Comfortable in the small kitchen now, he located the corkscrew, opened and filled two stemless red wine glasses, and joined her on the couch.

She accepted the glass, swirled the wine, and lifted it to her nose. She inhaled and hmmm'd in apparent approval before sipping the garnet colored liquid. Her eyes closed and her throat worked as she swallowed.

And once again, he was rock hard. He adjusted his pants and shifted away from her. He sampled the Rhone blend and the dark berry flavors exploded on his tongue.

"That's delicious, full-bodied enough without any hard edges." Okay, so they could sit and discuss wine, like two old friends. He reclined back into the soft cushions––allowing himself to finally relax.

Campbell turned to face him and tucked her long legs under her skirt. "Right?" Her earlier smile had faded.

"What's up?"

She squeezed her eyes shut for a moment and tucked her hair behind her ear. "I've got something to tell you and I think you'll be happy because I may have solved our dilemma."

"You found another apartment?" His throat tightened.

She bit her lip. "Not exactly, but I'm going to stay with Cam for a week or two in Monterey, so you'll have this place to yourself. I'm concerned about him, and I have some meetings there. By the time I get back, harvest should be winding down and another apartment should open up."

She paused and pasted on a wide smile. "You'll be fine at Maison du Soleil without me, right?"

The five-course gourmet meal solidified into a brick in his gut. Had he driven her away by sharing his feelings this morning? "And Cam agreed?"

"At first he accused me of checking up on him, but I told him I'd had trouble concentrating on my exam prep."

Jack pressed to his feet and strolled over to the kitchen. "That's probably a good idea. As long as you can meet with the potential chefs here, I've got the hotel handled." *Keep it about business.*

"It shouldn't be a problem to coordinate those meetings with Austin for when I return." Her voice was quiet.

He set his wineglass on the counter but kept his back toward her. "Well, I'll finally be able to sleep in a real bed, right?" He injected a careless note in his voice.

"And no more distractions or stress over someone dropping by, right?"

He glanced over his shoulder at and quirked an eyebrow. "Exactly. It makes sense and if anyone can assess how Cam is really doing, it's you. When are you going?"

She lowered her gaze to her clasped hands. "Sunday."

He picked up his wine and downed a mouthful. "I'll do my best to be out of here by the time you return. Keep me posted."

"Jack, this is the smart thing for both of us. And for Cam. Will you come back to the living room? We never finished watching *Princess Bride*."

Not a chance in hell—was she really so oblivious? His fingers tightened on his glass. No way could he cuddle on the couch and watch her favorite movie and pretend they were just buddies. Her decision was reasonable, but it didn't prevent the sharp tug in his chest.

He blew out a long exhale. "I'm really wiped out. Would you mind if I hit the sack? I've got an early morning at Maison du Soleil tomorrow." Might as well rip off the band-aid.

The silence sat heavy in the apartment. He angled toward her, leaning one elbow against the kitchen island.

A crease formed between her brows and she stood. "Of course. It is late."

Before she could come closer, he turned toward the bedroom. "Let me grab a few things from my dresser so I don't wake you up in the morning." Call him a coward.

"Jack."

"I'll just be a couple minutes." He closed the door behind him. Right now he was finished talking. Especially with her.

CAMPBELL LEANED a hip against the counter and massaged her temples. Her decision was rational. Logical. Campbell Taylor, the responsible sibling everyone could count on. So why was her stomach twisted into knots and her head pounding?

It had only been luck that they hadn't been discovered.

Jack hadn't batted even one long luxurious eyelash. He'd reverted into his usual easygoing charming guy-persona. The one where nothing appeared to ruffle his feathers. As if he couldn't care less she was leaving.

What had she expected? Him to plead with her to stay?

She busied herself with rinsing the wineglasses and setting them on the drying rack. What was he doing behind her closed bedroom door? And why did her heart ache knowing that it was probably the last time he'd ever be in her bedroom again?

His words from earlier today had touched her. The glimpses of his emotions he'd shared had etched themselves in her heart. Who was she kidding? Over the last month, her schoolgirl crush had morphed into love. Like, I love you, want to marry you and live happily ever after type of love. Leaving him now hurt.

Compartmentalization time. No need to burden Jack with her messy emotions, not when she was the one initiating the separation. What was the point of sharing her feelings? She was the one who needed to focus on studying. She was the one who was leaving.

It was for the best. No more glimpses of Jack in a damp towel. No more proximity to the bed where they'd slept spooned together in perfect harmony. No more intimate reminders of mind-blowing sex. When she returned, her apartment would be hers alone and they could return to being old friends and co-workers.

One day.

Hopefully.

They'd agreed it would be a one-time thing––they would remain friends. They'd agreed when it turned into a two-time thing––they would remain friends. So, even if her heart yearned for him, she would make sure they would remain friends. She'd survived her angsty teenaged crush, right?

No distance makes the heart grow fonder for her, more like out of sight, out of mind.

In two weeks, it would be like their hook up had never happened.

CHAPTER 20

$\mathcal{A}$gainst her better judgment, Campbell brewed another cup of coffee. If she had caffeine after 1 p.m., she'd be wide awake all night. Not like she'd had a restful night sleep since she'd been in Monterey. Cam had been swamped over at Cypress Coast Ranch, so she'd barely seen him except for some late take-out meals.

She hadn't spoken to Jack. Not once.

She pressed one hand to her churning belly––she'd gotten what she wanted so why did she feel so unsettled? They'd texted and emailed updates, but he'd been engrossed in the extensive preparations involved in opening the hotel. Their communications had been to-the-point, friendly, yet impersonal. Like two co-workers, nothing more.

She'd claimed Jack was a distraction, but here she was alone, and her focus was non-existent. She pulled out her planner and stared at the yawning expanse of blank pages for the rest of the week. Oh, the irony of wishing for a commitment-free schedule to study. As a student, she'd always been able to close off the external stimulation and hone in on what mattered. Not so much now--she had the attention span of a turnip.

The chrome espresso machine beeped, and she turned her attention to pouring the black brew into her Paris is for Lovers red mug. She would caffeinate, go for a thirty-minute walk along the breathtaking stretch of coast, and savor the heavy gray fog that cloaked the day. While Paso would get wisps of fog and clouds, it was known for its sunshine. Monterey, not so much. The perfect climate for her grumpy brother--he could prowl the coast like Heathcliff storming along the moors.

On one hand, she was thrilled to see that Cam was fully engaged in his role and didn't appear depressed. On the other hand, running away from the situation in Paso was amplifying her feelings and forcing her to face a few hard truths.

Instead of delving deeper into her studies, she'd turned inward and begun questioning her motivations. Could she truly only be fulfilled if she traveled after becoming a Master Sommelier? Was a far-flung locale what she required to feel her dreams had come true?

Was she seeking recognition for her own happiness or to prove something to the world?

Because restless nights had led to some unanticipated answers. Sure, a glamorous role in Europe would be incredible but her current role as Beverage Manager for Hotel Kings rocked. Not many people were lucky enough to work with family and a group of friends you respected and liked. Or have their family live within driving distance. She loved overseeing the programs for all the hotels, especially Maison du Soleil. Every single aspect of a Master Sommelier role could be fulfilled in Paso Robles.

Maybe her fascination with the possibility of being offered exotic global gigs was more ego-driven than anything else. Just like when she'd played soccer—she'd had to be the best. In school, she'd had to earn the best grades. Self-confidence was one thing, but would her life have been different if she'd been number two instead of number one? Because if being number one was the end game, why wasn't she hitting the books more and pining for Jack less?

Time apart proved isolating herself with her books didn't improve her concentration. Instead, she couldn't stop thinking about Jack. She missed the glimpses of sensitivity and sweetness that lay beneath his polished, self-possessed image. He'd let down his guard with her and the man beneath the charm was more appealing than her dreams could have fathomed.

Time apart flipped the floodlights on her feelings—she was in love with Jack Cassidy. Not that it was too far of a leap with their shared history, her longtime crush, and the mind-blowing sex. But it was deeper than that.

He'd shared his feelings with her about wanting to pursue a relationship under different circumstances and she'd clung to her need for achievement and fled. She'd simply been too scared to examine how her girlhood crush had morphed into real adult feelings. Did she have the courage to share them with Jack? She pressed the heels of her hands against her closed eyes.

Her phone rang and Xavier's name flashed on the screen—time for their weekly check-in call. They hadn't spoken since she'd left town.

"Hi Xavier." She crossed to the over-stuffed gray couch and sank into the cushions, her coffee cradled in her hands.

Her mentor's deep voice was brisk. "Campbell, how are you doing?"

Campbell stared at the black brew in her mug that reflected her mood. "I'm fine. I've had several uninterrupted hours to study." Technically true, although those hours hadn't been spent on deepening her wine expertise.

Xavier cleared his throat. "Well, that's good. Have you settled the issues at the Monterey property yet?"

She closed her eyes and blew out a breath. "It's going well." For the hotel anyway.

"Excellent news. You mentioned in your email update that you had some questions you wanted to discuss. Is now a good time?"

"It is." Campbell stared out at the enormous tree shading her brother's front yard. He'd rented an adorable three-bedroom house a few blocks from the hotel, with a peek ocean view. The yard was an explosion of colorful flowers, verdant shrubs, and a few huge evergreen trees that shrouded the property.

She exhaled a shaky breath. "I wanted to ask about whether it's realistic for me to expect part-time or temporary Master Sommelier offers next year or if most positions require a permanent move?"

He cleared his throat. "Funny you should ask because a few of my contacts reached out. They've heard about you through the grapevine and inquired about your plans after passing your exams next year."

"Through the grapevine, I see what you did there." Her heartrate kicked up, she set down her cup, and walked to the expansive picture window. "And what did you tell them?"

"I told them I believed you were an excellent candidate and could pick and choose where you want to go."

Her breath caught. "You did?"

He laughed. "Of course. You're my star, Campbell. I know you're committed to the Hotel Kings, which is an excellent position, but should you want some variety, there are part-time and consulting gigs you could consider, too."

"That's such a major compliment coming from you, Xavier, and it's everything I've worked so hard for over the last decade. Thank you." She pressed her hand to her throat.

"I give credit where credit is due. You've got a gift, Campbell. Now when will you be back because Sylvia does need you for group study?"

"I've got a few important interviews tomorrow. I was planning to return next week but I can come back after those." A twinge of guilt shot through her--she'd abandoned Sylvia.

Sure, part of her coming up was because of Cam but it was mostly to manage her confused feelings for her brother's best friend.

"Excellent. I've set up a few barrel tastings for you two on Friday, so that should be an easy transition back."

"You know I love barrel tastings." One of her favorite perks of the profession.

Xavier laughed. "I'll let them know you'll be back in time, and I'll send you the location details."

"Thank you so much. For all of it. See you on Friday."

After she tossed her phone onto the couch, she sank into the cushions. Overall, Xavier's call was everything she'd dreamed of--having the ability to pick positions and the honor of garnering attention before she'd passed her Master Sommelier exam. The ultimate pinnacle.

Now she had some decisions to make. Most people in her profession kept their personal lives simple for this very reason--it was a lot easier to pick up and move to France or Italy or Dublin when one was single. Her throat tightened and she clasped her hands together in her lap, digging her fingernails into her palms.

She was single. But did she want to be? If she bared her heart to Jack when she returned to Paso, would he want to date her? Or would they slide back into their pre-apartment sharing relationship. Old family friends. Colleagues. Platonic.

Her heart cracked in her chest. How would she be able to pretend she wasn't in love with him? Because it hadn't been only sex. Was she brave enough to find out if he felt the same way?

Because they hadn't spoken once, she had no idea if he'd want to try.

She had thirty-six hours to figure it out.

JACK TOWELED OFF AFTER A LONG, semi-scalding shower and hunted for a pair of sweats and some of the CBD ointment Campbell swore by for her lower back pain. His deltoids were on fire and his lower back was as stiff as an octogenarian's.

Why offering to help one of the sub-contractors carry heavy pallets had seemed like a good idea was a mystery. Granted, his decision-making process was negligible at best right now. Thank god he hadn't had any major contracts or other important documents to handle.

Simply put, somehow in less than a month with Campbell, she'd gone from being one of his favorite people to his person. He'd tumbled off a ledge and had no clue how to claw his way out of the hole.

Kick ass company started with his best friends and his dream career=check

Ideal location to live for foreseeable future=check

Learned he was capable of unconditionally loving one woman=check

So, what the hell did he do now? Somehow he'd always figured the first two ambitions would satisfy him. Give him true contentment without that restless itch that coursed through his veins.

Not so much. Of course, he loved his job, but he'd never been that guy who was defined by a title or who got his self-esteem from his Linked.in profile. As the last decade of what some might call job-hopping could attest. Frankly, it wasn't until Campbell that the falling in love and committing to one woman had been added to his checklist.

He loved her. He wanted her. He wanted to marry her and live happily ever after. And if anyone had ever told him he'd be waxing poetic about walking down the aisle, he probably would have cracked up. But here he was. And he couldn't discuss it with his brothers from another mother because it was a secret. He refused to betray Campbell's privacy.

A loud knock at the door interrupted his musings. He glanced down at his bare torso and ancient sweats, which would have to suffice. He didn't have any fucks to give.

He cracked the door and there stood Kyle, the landlord, a sheaf of papers in hand.

"Hey Kyle, what can I do for you?"

The short heavy-set man waved the documents. "Is it okay if I come in for a moment? I've got some news to share with you."

Jack opened the door fully and waved him in. "Sure." Because all he needed right now was to be reminded of how all of this had started. Then immediately felt like a callous jerk.

"So, how's your dad doing?"

Kyle blew out a breath. "He passed away a few days ago. Can we sit down?"

"Oh man, I'm so sorry. Can I get you anything? A glass of water? A beer?" Poor guy.

Kyle shook his head and sank onto one of the barstools by

the kitchen island. "No thanks. He was sick for a long time, and it was his time."

Not having a single clue what to say, Jack nodded.

"He went downhill about a week ago and he agreed we could move him to the ICU, so that's where he passed on. But I came because I wanted to thank both you and Campbell for your generosity in giving me those last few weeks with him close by."

Jack swallowed; his throat parched. "That was all Campbell."

"Well, I know you're a real estate attorney and you could have pushed the issue. So, thank you for that. I owe you. And the apartment has been cleaned and is ready for you now. I brought the lease agreement back and I'm giving you the next month at no charge. Okay?"

Jack stared at him for a moment, not fully processing. "Now?"

Kyle nodded. "I mean, unless you two want to stay here together instead?"

Why yes, yes I do. "Oh no, Campbell will be thrilled to have her space back. And my back thanks you. That Murphy bed is great for a few nights, but for long-term for a guy my size…"

"Yeah, it's more for weekend visitors. Okay, well here is the revised lease and the keys. You can move in right away." Kyle stood and glanced around. "Is Campbell here? I wanted to thank her in person."

Jack shook his head. "No, she's actually out of town for a few days. But I'll move my stuff over first thing in the morning. And I'm really sorry about your father."

"Thanks. It's tough but he had a great life." Kyle crossed to the door. "Let me know if you need anything."

After he left, Jack sank back onto the barstool. Well, their big dilemma was solved, right? He'd have his original place.

She'd have her own apartment. Nobody would ever have to know. He surveyed the apartment, little touches of Campbell everywhere.

The framed family photo on her tiny desk, special vintage bottles on the counter above the wine refrigerator, the floral scent of her hair somehow still permeating the space despite her almost two-week absence. This was what he wanted, right?

So why did he feel like drowning his sorrows in the bottle of MacLellan?

Maybe one glass would take the edge off. He pulled the bottle from the cabinet, found a tumbler glass, and poured a few fingers. He wasn't the kind of guy to drink alone, but special occasions and all that. He rolled his eyes, headed to the couch and downed a mouthful.

He should let Campbell know but they'd only communicated via text and email--impersonal as hell. Not exactly the best way to inform her he'd be gone when she returned. But he wasn't ready to talk to her, either. Yeah, he was a coward. So what? He'd let her know before she returned.

Tomorrow, he'd pack his bag and move across the courtyard, where he should have been from the beginning.

Tonight, he'd sleep between her sheets one last time, pathetic bastard that he was.

CHAPTER 21

Campbell swallowed the nerves bubbling in her throat. Her brother had insisted on accompanying her back to Paso Robles to meet with the Maison du Soleil architect about some renovation questions for the Monterey hotel.

Of course, her brother decided they must stop by her place first and drive out to the hotel together so he could ride back with Jack. Her gut twisted imagining that conversation.

For the entire drive--separately, thank goodness--she'd been stressing out about Cam seeing something of Jack's in her condo. For the tenth time, she texted Jack--*just reply for god's sake*--with zero response. She smacked her palm on the steering wheel.

She parked in front of her place and Cam parked his navy Jeep Cherokee next to her. Jack's SUV wasn't there, so at least they wouldn't walk into him stepping out of the shower buck naked or something. She ran her tongue around her teeth, recalling exactly when that happened before.

She shook her head and stepped out of her car. Time to dump her suitcase, change out of her sweats into something at least semi-professional to go on-site, and pray that Jack hadn't left his boxers out. If he hadn't read her messages, he might not know she had returned.

Cam walked over by her trunk and insisted on taking her suitcase. "Let me get it, I know your back bugs you after driving sometimes."

She smiled at her brother. "It's actually doing pretty good right now, but thanks for remembering." *It didn't even act up much after your best friend and I had wild monkey sex against the wall.*

Heat rose to her cheeks, and she hurried up the path and unlocked the front door. She scanned the open living space––and the apartment was pristine. She blew out a breath, her nerves scaling down a notch.

Cam followed her inside and placed her suitcase next to her beloved plum-colored velvet sofa. "Great place, but man it's tiny."

"It's the perfect size for me right now. Less to keep clean." She set her leather satchel onto the quartz countertop. "There's filtered water in the fridge. Give me a minute to change."

"No worries, I've got to hit the bathroom before we go." Cam started to cross the room.

She sucked in a sharp inhale. "Can you wait one second? I'm going to die if I don't pee first." She sped around the kitchen island and beat him to the door.

What if Jack's shaving supplies or Jack's anything at all was in the bathroom?

He held up both hands. "Geez, go ahead."

She gave a sheepish grin and called over her shoulder. "Sorry, bladder the size of a walnut."

Once she closed and locked the door, she checked the shower and the medicine cabinet. No menthol shaving cream. No razor. No toothbrush. Not a sign of Jack. She crouched down and opened the cabinet underneath the sink and again, only her toiletries.

Had he found a new place and not told her? Would he actually bail without telling her first? Not that he owed her an explanation. It was always the plan he'd move out as soon as a place became available, but it would be polite at least let her know, right?

Had he been angry with her and seen through her excuses to leave? They hadn't talked in nearly two weeks so maybe he didn't feel he needed to tell her? Her heart clenched in her chest. Had they already become so detached?

She jolted when Cam knocked on the door. "Hey, your landlord is at the door, and I really need to get in there."

"Coming." The color drained from her face, and she splashed some cold water on her cheeks. She fumbled with the doorknob and prayed Cam had been his usual gruff self and not chatted with Kyle.

When she re-entered the living room, Kyle stood right inside the door. "Hey Campbell, I saw your car and wanted to check in with you."

"Of course, let's talk outside." Out of her brother's hearing range.

His eyes widened behind his glasses, but he followed her onto her small porch. "Is it a bad time?"

She shook her head. "No, no. I'm sorry. I've been in the car for a few hours and wanted to feel the sun on my face." She winced, was that the best she could come up with?

"Well, like I told Jack the other day, I wanted to make sure I thanked you in person for everything you did. It meant a lot to have my dad here before he passed."

She frowned. "Oh no, I didn't know your father passed away. I'm so sorry."

"Jack didn't tell you?" He tilted his head, his brows drawn together.

"No, we haven't spoken in the last few days. We've both been really busy. And he's not home right now." Thank god.

Kyle scratched his jaw. "You know he moved into the other apartment a few days ago, right? I stopped by and gave Jack the keys."

"Again, I'm so sorry to hear about your father. And like I mentioned, Jack and I have both been really busy and haven't been able to connect. My condolences to you and your family."

He nodded and stepped back. "Your generosity made a big difference for us. Thank you again for offering to share your place with Jack. Let me know if you need anything at all."

"Of course. Take care." When Kyle turned and crossed the courtyard, Campbell blew out an unsteady breath.

It was a lot to unpack. Jack had moved out without a word. If that wasn't a major statement, she didn't know what was. Had he been planning on telling her? Or just let her figure it out when she found no trace of him remained in her condo?

Would he have left this way if she'd responded to him sharing his feelings before she went to Monterey? Her vision blurred and she blinked furiously to stave off tears. No way would she cry about this situation and certainly not in front of her perceptive brother.

"That seemed like a serious conversation. Everything okay?" Cam's quiet voice murmured from behind her.

She jumped and turned toward the now open door. How long had he been standing there?

"Yes, it was. His father passed away while I was up in Monterey. He'd been ill a long time."

Cam's brows lifted. "That's why he stopped by here? Had you met his father or something?"

She shook her head. "We'd discussed that his dad was

entering hospice care." Time to get out of here before Cam started asking more questions she didn't want to answer. "Anyway, let me change my clothes really quick, grab my bag, and I'll drive us to Maison du Soleil."

She brushed by him and fought to regulate her pounding heart. Her brother always liked to be in the know. Not this time. If he'd heard what Kyle said about Jack, he'd call her on it.

Her bed was neatly made and the second dresser no longer stood next to hers. Had Jack slept in her bed or the Murphy bed? Would her sheets carry a hint of his clean, crisp scent? Before she went and sniffed her pillow, she turned to the closet and seized the first dress her hands landed on.

After a quick change into a cobalt blue sundress, she grabbed her messenger bag and rushed outside. Her brother was on the phone, leaning against the passenger door of her car. She unlocked the doors and they climbed inside.

He powered off the phone. "That was Ryan. Said he'd like to join in the interview with your two chef candidates next week, too."

"That's a great idea, especially since it's our first hotel with a restaurant. Maybe if both candidates are great, we could consider offering one of them Monterey?"

Cam shrugged. "Maybe. But your place is more French farm-to-table and mine will be more California cuisine or Asian Fusion." He gazed out the window at the golden hills whizzing by. "Damn this is beautiful country."

Highway 46 was a winding road dotted with breathtaking vistas, impressive wineries, and pure gorgeous nature. "It really is fabulous."

Her brother flipped on the satellite radio and Adele's one-of-a-kind voice belted out "Someone Like You", a song that always made Campbell's heart ache with its melancholy beauty. And boy did it fit right now. But why would Cam leave this one on?

"Cam? You really want to listen to Adele?" She injected a teasing note into her voice.

He frowned. "Yeah, you got a problem with that?"

She shook her head. "Nope, just unexpected, that's all. We're almost there." Her brother never failed to surprise her.

JACK POWERED down his laptop and removed his noise-canceling earbuds. Not that they silenced the hammering and drilling, but they relegated the renovation sounds to background noise. In some ways, it was a comforting sound during the day, a reminder of the hotel's ongoing progress.

His phone buzzed and Cam's name flashed on the screen. He checked the message, *We're here. Where are you?*

He scrolled through several missed calls and texts from Campbell and a few from her brother. *Crap.* They were on site? He'd been buried in a few contract deadlines and hadn't checked his phone this morning. Not that the hotel's less than stellar connectivity had been corrected yet.

He scrubbed his hands across his face and rose from his chair and makeshift desk that he'd set up in one of the future luxury suites. Nerves jumped in his stomach—Campbell was here.

Meet you in the foyer.

How had he missed that the Taylors would be at the hotel today? He winced. Maybe he'd done too good of a job compartmentalizing and immersing himself in the hotel. He strode down the broad hallway, his heart racing—and there she stood, framed in the open doorway, a halo of sunlight shimmering around her. His throat constricted.

He forced an easy grin and stopped when he reached

them. "Sorry guys, it's like the wild west around here. I just saw your texts, Campbell."

"That's cool. I snagged a meeting with your architect about some design issues in Monterey. And my sister's babysitting assignment is over." Cam's lips twitched, softening his comment.

Campbell smacked her brother's arm. "Oh please, like anybody could get you in line." She lifted her cerulean eyes to Jack's. "And I was ready to get back. I missed Paso Robles."

"Did you get ahead on your studies?" His eyes widened. She missed Paso?

She shrugged but didn't look away. "Sort of. I definitely had time to think while I was away."

Something tightened in Jack's chest. "Good, that's good."

Cam waved a hand. "Hey guys, I'm supposed to meet Brad out by the pool area. Can you send me in the right direction and meet me after you play catch up?"

"Sorry, man. Go down the hall and turn left and you'll run into it." Jack pointed toward the outdoor lounge area.

"I'll see you guys in a bit." Cam turned and walked off.

"So." He drank her in, from the top of her shiny blonde head, down to the way her diamond-cut calves were shown to perfection in her high heels. He swallowed.

"How've you been?" Campbell's voice was tentative.

He shoved his hands into his pockets. "Really busy. More important, tell me about Cam. How is he?"

"Why don't we walk the property, you can update me on how everything's progressing, and I'll fill you in." Her lips curved upwards.

"Sure, let's head over to the restaurant, they've made some big strides there." They ambled down the open hall together, the floral scent from her hair making his fingers itch to free it from her ponytail.

"Well, he was at the hotel non-stop and he's really into it.

I mean, *all in*, which made me really happy. And personally he seems to be doing okay. I think being in charge is giving him purpose."

Jack nodded. "That's great news. I know how he feels. I didn't realize this place would become so important, so fast."

She tilted her head. "You really love it, don't you?"

"Yeah, yeah I do. It's not like the attorney work--which a lot of times feels like it's all about money or outsmarting the other side. Being part of renovating and creating Maison du Soleil feels like I'm building something instead of taking something apart." He rubbed the back of his neck. "Sorry to go on like that."

She reached out and stroked his arm. Every muscle leapt to attention, and he managed not to flex his biceps like some preening rooster. "I love seeing you so invested in it. That means it's your passion. That this is your place."

"I love it here. And I love the whole process--I get how Ryan felt about Pacific Jewel Inn more now. It's different when you're the one managing it all. It'll be great when the guys come up next month and I can't wait to go lend a hand on the other properties, too." The hotel business was in his blood now.

They reached the wide doorway into what would be Chez Paul Marc and Campbell clapped her hands together. "They've installed the bar and the chef's kitchen. Do they have the booths yet?"

Her excitement was contagious--he grinned. "I know I questioned you on the rose velvet booths and the mid-century modern white marble bar, but you were right. It's going to look incredible in here."

She pumped a fist in the air. "Aha, once again you're having to admit I'm right. I love it. And yes, it's going to look like an old school Parisian bistro."

"And once we hire the chef and they get rolling on the menu..."

"And the brilliant sommelier finishes curating the opening day wines." She spun in a wide circle, her face glowing. "It will be perfect. And I'm sorry I wasn't here to do more."

She caught her lower lip in her white teeth. "Jack, you said some things to me before I left, and I didn't really answer you. But I had a lot of time to think about it while I was away."

"I told you I didn't expect--" His shoulders tensed.

She held up a hand. "Let me say a few things. Please."

He glanced around the room, satisfied they were alone. "Okay."

She squared her shoulders. "You know I'm not great at talking about my feelings. But I've been so laser-focused on this damn exam and becoming a Master Som, I got tunnel vision. I lost some perspective wanting to be the best. Stepping away for a little bit helped me realize how much I love this job with Hotel Kings. How I'm lucky to work with my brother and you, and now my parents will be less than two hours away. That it doesn't have to be so black or white."

"Black or white?" He held his breath.

Her ice blue eyes widened. "I don't know. I think I believed when I attain Master Sommelier, I should take a gig abroad or seek out a Michelin Star restaurant or whatever. To prove to the people like Roger and the doubters that I'm good enough. To show everyone I'm a success.

But this restaurant will earn a Michelin Star, if Austin and I and the chef have anything to say about it. But even if it doesn't, I realized I'm grateful for what I already have."

"You're saying you want to stay in Paso Robles?" *With me?*

She nodded. "Well, this is where I want to be now. And I want to focus on living every day fully, not just working toward some day. I want to be all in, not just partially. Also, my mentor told me about consulting gigs and temporary contract positions that could be an option. Nothing is set in stone."

Warmth spread through him. "Campbell, that's awesome. And you don't need to prove what a badass you are to anyone. You just *are.*"

She hesitated a moment and then wound her arms around his neck. "Takes one to know one. And one more thing." Her warm breath tickled the hollow of his throat.

His arms banded around her waist. "Yeah?"

She leaned her head back and gazed up at him, her eyes serious. "I realized it's not only the place. I want to be with you."

His heart slammed against his chest. "Be with me? What are you saying?"

"That life is really short. And because I am a badass and you are a badass, we should be able to have a personal life and be badass at all of it, right?" Her brows lifted.

Adrenaline coursed through his veins. "Are you sure?"

She nodded, a flush staining her chiseled cheekbones. "I'm terrified. But I've had a crush on you since I was fifteen years old and I'm crazy about you. I'm scared I'll mess this up but if you still want to try, I want to."

"Yes, I want you." He captured her mouth, her sweet breath melded with his, and she arched her slender body into him. He slid his hand down, rocking her hips into the ridge of his arousal.

She nipped at his bottom lip. "How soon can we get out of here?"

He growled and stroked his hands up her back, one hand catching her ponytail and tugging her head back. "Not until later, damn it. Tell me Cam isn't staying over."

She gasped and stepped back. "Oh crap, I totally forgot about Cam. Do you think he'll freak out?"

Someone cleared their throat from the room's entrance. "Freak out about what? My best friend with his hands all over my baby sister's ass?"

Jack jolted but didn't retreat. "Cam, I--"

Campbell whirled around to face her brother. "Cam, it's not what it looks like."

Cam crossed his arms over his chest. "Do you guys think I'm blind? I could tell something was up that night at dinner with Mom and Dad."

"Seriously?" Campbell put her hands on her hips.

He smirked. "Sis, you gave the waitress a death glare when she was checking Jack out. And you were moping around Monterey like a lovesick puppy."

"Hey." Campbell's jaw dropped. "I did not."

"Did so. Anyway, don't put me in the middle of anything. You're grown-ass adults so maybe don't make out in the middle of the hotel. And don't screw each other over. Brad wanted to speak to all of us together, so meet me over there in five." He pivoted and marched away.

For a moment, Campbell stared at her brother's retreating form, then they both burst out laughing.

Jack shrugged. "So I guess we don't need to worry about your big brother beating me up."

She linked one arm in his. "He told us, didn't he?"

Jack grinned, a lightness pouring through him. "So, you were glaring at the waitress, huh? Ready to defend your turf?"

She snorted and bumped his hip. "Defend my turf--cocky much? C'mon Cassidy, no slacking on the job. Let's go."

"I kind of like the idea you're jealous and possessive. Who

would've believed you'd be that way?" His grin had morphed into shit-eating territory and he was fine with it.

"I'm never going to hear the end of this, am I?" She blushed and rolled her eyes.

He hugged her in close, savoring the warmth of her skin and her soft curves pressed into his side. "Not on my watch."

CHAPTER 22

*wo weeks later*

"Why do I need to come back up to the hotel tonight? Can't it wait? I just got home an hour ago." Campbell frowned.

"It really can't. This chandelier was custom made for the wine cave, the designer showed up a day early, she's leaving on a red-eye tonight to return to New York, and insists on your personal stamp of approval first." Jack's whiskey-smooth voice was apologetic.

"Seriously? But can't you show me on the phone?" She glanced down at her navy and white striped sports bra and matching capris. Her yoga plans were in jeopardy. "That should be good enough."

Jack hissed. "Look, you insisted this woman was the only one to create the chandelier and you knew her reputation. *Please.* She scares me. I swear she might rip it out of the ceiling and take it with her if you don't."

Campbell gazed longingly at her yoga mat and the special bottle of 2018 Villa Creek Avenger breathing in her crystal decanter. So much for her vino and vinyasa plans. It would have to be vino and dinner with Jack when they returned from Maison du Soleil.

"Fine. This sounds melodramatic, if you ask me. I'm in my workout clothes and I'm not changing. I'll be there in twenty." And if the designer thought she was a slob, too damn bad.

"Great. And I'm not telling you to break the speed limit but if you could hurry, I would appreciate it." Strain threaded through his smooth voice.

"I'll be there as soon as I can. Our wine is decanting and it's your turn to pick up dinner."

"Of course, I'll take care of it. See you soon." His tone could melt butter.

She stalked to her room, threw on a flowy tangerine colored tank top--showing up in her sports bra might be too much--and grabbed her messenger bag. Irritation fueled her strides to her Volvo. The chandelier better be worthy of hanging in the Louvre.

On the drive to York Mountain, she blasted some Cage the Elephant, singing at the top of her lungs. Their funky indie rock sound never failed to lift her mood. Although tonight's return trip to the hotel was a pain in the butt, seeing Jack an hour sooner than planned wasn't a hardship.

Over the last few weeks, they'd settled into a rhythm of hectic, work-packed days and sensual nights either at her condo or his. As she'd predicted--hoped--being with Jack wasn't a distraction. Actually, it was the opposite. She was more productive with her studying and work duties because she was motivated to be as efficient as possible. More time to savor him. Go figure.

She navigated the twists and turns and reached Maison

du Soleil in record time. The sooner she signaled her approval, the sooner they could hurry home and she could pounce on him. She simply couldn't get enough of him––in bed and out.

After crossing across the gravel and stone walkway, she hurried down what would be the hotel's main hallway toward the wine cellar. *Her* wine cellar. The above-ground room was already going to be one-of-a-kind and the chandelier was the focal point for the space, well, besides all the wine displays that would line the room.

She reached the wine cave, gasped, and lifted her hands to cover her mouth. A massive, tiered masterpiece, with layers of sparkling crystal, and a bold mid-century classic vibe was suspended from the middle of the ceiling. It bathed the large room in a golden glow that highlighted the exposed brick and gleaming hardwood floors.

Jack stepped out of the shadows and caught one hand. "Do you love it?"

She turned into the circle of his arms and threw her arms around his neck. "It is gorgeous. Wow wow wow. Daniela outdid herself."

He hugged her close and the fine hairs on the back of her neck prickled––her entire body leaping to attention. "Yeah, I think it's worth every penny."

She stiffened and gazed around the room. "Where's Daniela? This is beyond what I could have envisioned. And I can't believe you got it installed this afternoon."

Jack raised one hand to her jaw and gently turned her face. "About that. Um, she's not here."

Her eyes widened. "What do you mean? You told me I had to get out here pronto and I did."

"Yeah, well, I told you that because I wanted to surprise you." He smiled, his crystalline eyes crinkling at the corners.

"Surprise me?" She searched the chiseled planes of his face, the softness in his expression.

"You're so beautiful." He skimmed his hand lightly along her cheek and clasped her chin. His eyes hooded and he lowered his perfect sculpted mouth to hers, brushing her lips in a whisper-soft kiss.

"Jack." His name escaped on a sigh.

With a growl low in his throat, he deepened the kiss, his tongue stroking along hers, tasting of red wine and his unique flavor. A tenderness permeated their embrace, a languid softness without their usual urgency. Like they had all the time in the world.

After a few satisfying moments, he lifted his head, his dilated pupils almost obscuring the pale green irises. "I missed you."

Her lips twitched. "You saw me two hours ago and I was here all day."

He quirked one dark brow. "And your point?"

"You're silly. So, if Daniela isn't here, what's my surprise?" She stepped back and scanned the room, then froze. A round white-tablecloth-covered table sat in the middle of the room, adorned with fancy silver-domed covered plates and glistening crystal champagne flutes.

He placed one broad hand on her lower back and guided her toward the table. "I told you I had dinner handled, didn't I?"

"I thought you meant Chinese take-out?" She angled her head toward him.

He leaned down and pressed a light kiss on her lips. "Surprise. We've been working a lot and I wanted to get the chandelier installed early and celebrate."

He pulled out a burgundy cloth-covered chair and she sank into the soft cushions. "That's really sweet of you." Her breath hitched and her heart took a slow-diving roll.

He flashed a charming grin and brandished a bottle of Veuve and filled their glasses. "I am sweet, aren't I?"

She giggled. "And so modest, too." And damn if she didn't love his confidence and sense of humor. "I propose a toast to the sweetest man in Paso Robles."

He pressed a hand to his broad chest. "Just Paso Robles?"

She rolled her eyes and lifted her glass. "The sweetest man in the whole universe. Is that better?"

He clinked her glass and sat down across from her. "More like it."

She savored the crisp chilled bubbles sliding down her throat. "Mmm…delicious. Thank you. Although I feel I'm under-dressed for champagne."

He shook his head. "Never. And you're dressed perfectly. I got one of your old favorites for dinner. Look and see."

She lifted the lid. "Oh yum, I haven't had a pot pie in forever." Her eyes closed, she inhaled the aroma, and her mouth watered.

"Your mom always made them the day after Thanksgiving, and they were my favorite, too. This one is chicken, but I figured it would do the trick." He beamed.

Her stomach grumbled and she picked up her fork. "Okay, this is an amazing surprise. Thank you."

For a few minutes, they dug into the delicious meal, the crispy crust complementing the creamy sauce, tender chunks of chicken, and tasty vegetables. Each bite reminded her of home. Jack's thoughtfulness touched her heart.

His light green eyes gleamed beneath the twinkling light. "Worth driving back up here, right?"

"Absolutely. And you're staying over at my place tonight, right?" She winked.

He shook his head. "Will you stay with me tonight?"

She shrugged. "Sure, but my bed is more comfy than yours." Not that she planned on letting him get much sleep.

He leaned forward, reached across the table, and clasped her hand, intertwining his long fingers with hers. "Campbell, I've thought about how to say this and I'm just going to say it, okay?"

Her breath caught in her throat, and she nodded. "Okay."

He exhaled and squeezed her hand. "I know it's only been a short time, well I mean we've known each other a long time, but the way I feel about you now is new and different and amazing."

"Jack––" The fine hairs on the back of her neck prickled and her pulse thrummed in her throat.

He squeezed her fingers again. "Campbell, you're the most incredible person I've ever met. Your passion, your drive, your love for your family, your big brain all blow me away. But it's your heart that's woken up mine in a way I never thought possible. I love you."

Joy shimmered through her, and she leapt to her feet, circling around to him. "I love you, too. I've been in love with you from the moment I met you."

He tugged her down onto his lap and she grabbed his handsome face in both hands and planted an open-mouthed kiss on him. "Tell me again."

He chuckled and murmured against her lips, "I love you, Campbell Taylor."

"I love you. But can we stay at my place?" Every nerve in her body sang and she melted against his hard hot body.

He lifted his head. "What if I told you that I found an incredible rental house and bought a California King bed that I guarantee you'll want to sleep in with me?"

"You found a place? I didn't know you'd been looking." Harvest was winding down, so it made sense. But she liked having him mere steps across the courtyard.

His lips twitched. "Well, it's surprise number two but I won't sign the lease if you don't want to."

Her eyes widened. "If I don't want to?"

"Will you move in with me? And if you don't like this house, we can look for something else. But I want to be with you. Not waste any more time."

Her heart flip-flopped and heat curled down her spine. "I thought you wanted to wait and buy a place? Plant roots?"

"I do. I mean, I am. Everything's going great here at the hotel. I love Paso. But I know you're still not sure if you'll stay here long-term, so I figured renting a house for a year would be smarter."

She searched his face, where an unfamiliar hint of vulnerability glinted in his green eyes. She pressed her palm against his solid chest, the staccato beat of his heart steadying her. "Yes. I'd love to move in with you. And I love that you found a rental first, just in case. But I know I want to be with you and wherever you are is home. Even if we both end up traveling for work, we'll come home to each other."

His eyes lit up and his voice was husky. "You are home for me, Campbell. I love you so much."

Her lips curved up and she wiggled in his lap, the steel ridge of his arousal digging into her. "Let's get out of here. My place? For old time's sake?"

"Your place tonight and then ours every night from now on." He swooped down and kissed her.

After a few satisfying minutes, they rose from the chair. "I'll race you back to my condo." Campbell caught his hand and pulled.

"Did I mention that's another quality of yours I love?" They rushed from the wine cellar toward the parking lot.

"That I drive fast?" She laughed.

He winked. "No, that you're insatiable."

Heat rose in her cheeks. "I mean, have you looked in the mirror lately?"

"You just want me for my body?" He batted his eyelashes.

Elation flowed through her. "I want you because you're the man of my dreams."

He pulled her into his embrace and slanted his mouth across hers. "You're mine."

They leapt in their cars and returned to the condo where it all began. Together.

EPILOGUE

$\mathcal{M}$aison du Soleil, Opening Gala, New Year's Eve

JACK STOOD at wine cellar's entrance and surveyed the room--warmth filling him. How had he ever considered it a dark cave? Sparkling lights adorned the perimeter, reflecting down on the clusters of guests gathered throughout the space. The buzz of lively conversations and the clinking of wineglasses melded perfectly with the string quartet playing at the far end of the room.

The entire Hotel Kings team, several of the local winery owners and winemakers, and the first round of Maison du Soleil guests all appeared to be having a great time. Campbell, along with their new chef Angus, had created a paired wine and tasting menu, which was set up on a long buffet table. His parents, who had followed through and shown up for the grand opening, chatted with the Taylors, Campbell's mentor and friend Sylvia, and Campbell, who was looking striking in a slim ruby red dress.

Her gaze found him from across the room and her full lips, painted the same dangerous shade as her dress, curved upward. She stole his breath.

Without breaking eye contact, she excused herself and sauntered toward him on those long, toned legs that never failed to drive him wild. His body leapt to attention, and he willed himself to act cool. They had a long evening ahead of them.

When she reached him, she stretched up and pressed a light kiss on his lips. "Hi handsome, you look lonely standing alone over here, want to get a room?"

He wrapped one arm around her and hugged her to his side. "We've got the Presidential suite tonight and I've got *The Princess Bride* teed up for us since we still haven't finished watching it. I'll meet you there next year."

She giggled and placed one hand over his heart. "It's a deal. Only two hours and fifteen minutes to go. And I'm so glad we're all staying out here tonight. Everything's going really well. I'm so proud of you. And so are all the parents."

He lifted his wineglass and toasted her. "I'm proud of you and I couldn't have done it without you by my side. Congratulations on acing your exam. You're one step closer to achieving your dreams."

Her eyes darkened. "Being with you is a dream come true. Not my teenaged fantasy of how it would be with the gorgeous Jack Cassidy, but real-life dream of finding my perfect partner. You helped me figure out that every step of the journey is what it's all about, not only the end result. You make me the happiest woman in the world."

His chest tightened. "What a coincidence because you make me the happiest man in the world. And I'd planned on waiting until we're alone in our suite, but I can't wait another minute."

Her eyes widened. "Wait?"

"Hold my wine?" He handed her the glass and reached one hand into his pocket.

"Jack?"

He dropped to one knee, flicked open the eggshell blue velvet box, and offered it to her. "Campbell Taylor, I love you. The last few months you've shown me how incredible life can be. No matter where we go or what we do, as long as you're with me, I'm home. Will you marry me?"

She lifted her hands to her face, then laughed when she realized she was double fisted with two full glasses of wine. She bent and placed them on the floor. "I will absolutely marry you. Will you put the ring on for me?"

He stood and slid the sparkling oval cut solitaire on her slender finger. She held it up her hand. "It's perfect. I love you so much, Jack."

She threw her arms around his neck, and he picked her up and spun her around, joy filling him.

A man coughed next to them. "It's the grand opening gala, not a Hallmark movie of the week."

The Hotel Kings, Ryan, Austin, Cam, Lucas, Charlie, and their assistant Jon had materialized next to them. Jack hadn't even noticed.

"Whatever. You're jealous." Campbell smacked her brother on the shoulder. "I thought you'd be happy for us."

Cam's lips quirked. "Hey, I am. And now Mom won't pester me about getting married. But it's more fun to give you a hard time."

"Sorry Campbell, but Jack gave me so much crap about Charlie, it's only fair to return the favor. Congratulations." Ryan gave a crooked grin.

Charlie nodded her gorgeous blonde head. "That he did. Fair play and all that. Congrats you two."

Jon grinned and lifted his glass. "Is there going to be an engagement every time a hotel opens? I love you two together. Congratulations. And this place is incredible. I didn't think you'd be able to top Pacific Jewel Inn but Hotel Kings Property Number Two rocks."

Jack clinked his glass with Jon's. "Thanks, it does rock. Now it's Cam's turn."

"You can get engaged for me, Jon. I'll stick with opening Cypress Coast Ranch." Cam held up a hand.

"Never say never," Ryan said, then turned to Jack. "I know you asked me to give the welcome speech tonight, Jack, but I think you should do it. This is your baby."

Campbell squeezed his biceps. "Yes, you give the speech."

"If you insist. But let's wait until closer to midnight. I'm stoked everyone's having a great time and we finished on schedule." He smiled at his friend and hugged Campbell in closer to his side, contentment filling him.

"Well, I wasn't going to bring this up tonight but seeing as we've now got two weddings to plan, I better." Charlie's brows knit together.

"What's going on?" Ryan stepped closer to his fiancé.

Charlie grimaced. "Well, earlier today the wedding planner we hired for Cypress Coast Ranch informed me she got an 'offer she couldn't refuse,' in Maui and quit before she started." She made air quotes.

Cam frowned. "Are you kidding me? We're already fully booked with weddings through next Fall."

Charlie rolled her shoulders back and exhaled. "Well, it's not all bad. She mentioned a good friend who can step in. But now we need to interview this Lucy Goodwin person and make sure she's a fit."

"Lucy Goodwin?" Campbell's eyes went wide as dinner plates.

"Lucy Goodwin? No way," Cam barked and stumbled back a step.

Everyone stared at Cam. He pivoted and strode away, his limp more pronounced than usual.

"No way? What's going on?" Charlie put her hands on her hips. "You know her?"

Jack cleared his throat. "That's probably not going to work out, Charlie." *No way in hell.*

Campbell shook her head. "She was Cam's high school sweetheart. They were going to get married but he broke up with her before he left for the Middle East."

"Maybe working with Lucy is exactly what Cam needs. She was the one person who could bring out his lighter side," Ryan said.

Jack wasn't so sure. He and Campbell had found their happy ending, but Cam wasn't the same man who chose the army over the love of his life all those years ago

"For all we know, it's not an issue for Lucy––it's been years. Does she know Cam is running Cypress Coast Ranch?" Campbell asked.

Charlie shrugged. "No clue. So, is hiring her an option or do we have to start from scratch? That's going to be a real problem."

"This late in the game? We may have no choice." Ryan's expression darkened.

"Well, we don't need to figure this out tonight, right? Let's toast to the Hotel Kings and Maison du Soleil and Jack and me getting married." Campbell stepped into Jack's arms and raised her champagne flute. "Happy New Year's."

Jack hugged her close and lifted his glass. Everything he needed to be happy was in this room, most of all Campbell.

WHAT'S NEXT

Thank you for reading *Wine Country King*! I hope you loved Jack and Campbell's story as much as I loved writing it. And if you have a moment, please leave a review for *Wine Country King* on your favorite book site.

Ready for Cameron and Lucy's second chance/grumpy sunshine love story? **Monterey King** is avaialable now!

****

If you haven't read the Pacific Vista Ranch series, start with Sam and Holt's enemies to lovers romance, *Nobody Else But You.*

ACKNOWLEDGMENTS

As always, writing a book is a team effort. I'm so grateful for the assistance I received from so many fabulous people. Writing a story set in my favorite California wine region, Paso Robles, was a dream come true. My husband and I fell in love with the area and the wines years ago so, of course, we had to make a few "research" trips. For accuracy. *Ahem.*

While researching this book, my yoga teaching world intersected with my author life in an incredible way. A former yoga student happens to be one of the handful of women Master Sommeliers in the world––Laura Williamson. She was kind and generous enough to spend time sharing her journey with me, as well as insider information on the competitive Master Sommelier field.

One of my favorite wineries is Epoch Winery in Paso Robles. Jordan Fiorentini is their celebrated head winemaker and when she agreed to share her insights with me, we discovered she regularly takes my Yogadownload.com online yoga classes. Small world! Any errors on anything to do with wine are my mistakes!

I want to thank my wonderful beta readers: Kay Bennett, Joanna Kelly, Sara Martin, and Donna Simonetta—your individualized feedback helps me shape the final version of the story more than you could imagine. I appreciate your time and opinions. Big thanks to Katie O'Sullivan and Brenda St.

John Brown for helping me write the blurb. I also want to thank Walter Thomas for speaking with me about dating perspectives from the military point of view. This whole series was helped along by Lisa Ann Ray and her expertise in the luxury hotel space.

For the lovely author friends I've made along the way, with whom I share such a sense of camaraderie, thanks for being there: Donna Simonetta, Anna Bradley, Krista Sandor, Serena Bell, Christina Hovland, Liana de la Rosa, Katie O'Sullivan, Kerrigan Byrne, Charlotte O'Shay, Katie Baldwin, and many more. Especially over the last few years—I'd be lost without our online connection.

To my wonderful editor, Lindsey Faber, thank you for your brilliance! I don't know how I finished books before you. Thank you to Shasta Shafer for your eagle-eyed proofreading. Thank you Christina Hovland for this gorgeous cover—you are one talented woman.

Last but not least, to Todd for being my very own hero. I love you. And, finally to my furry kids: Lola, Beau, Josie, and Daisy, thanks for providing me daily laughs and all the cuddles.

ABOUT THE AUTHOR

Claire Marti is an award winning and *USA Today* Bestselling author of swoonworthy Contemporary Romance novels set in Southern California, including the Pacific Vista Ranch series and spin-off California Suits series. She lives in San Diego with her husband, silly dog, and three clever cats.

Claire started writing stories as soon as she was old enough to pick up pencil and paper. After graduating from the University of Virginia with a BA in English Literature, Claire was sidetracked by other careers, including practicing law, selling software for legal publishers, and managing a non-profit animal rescue for a Hollywood actress.

Finally, Claire followed her heart and now focuses on two of her true passions: writing romance and teaching yoga.